GET ALL
WITH JUST ONE P...

$50 VALUE

◆ **Hotel Discounts**
    up to 60%
    at home
    and abroad
        ◆ **Travel Service** -
    Guaranteed lowest published
    airfares plus 5% cash back on
    tickets ◆ **$25 Travel Voucher**
        ◆ **Sensuous Petite Parfumerie**
            collection ◆ **Insider
                Tips Letter** with
            sneak previews of
        upcoming books

You'll get a FREE personal card, too.
It's your passport to all these benefits– and to
even more great gifts & benefits to come!

There's no club to join. No purchase commitment. No obligation.

SD-PP5A

Enrollment Form

☐ *Yes!* I WANT TO BE A *Privileged Woman*.
Enclosed is one *PAGES & PRIVILEGES™* Proof of
Purchase from any Harlequin or Silhouette book currently for
sale in stores (Proofs of Purchase are found on the back pages
of books) and the store cash register receipt. Please enroll me
in *PAGES & PRIVILEGES™*. Send my Welcome Kit and FREE
Gifts -- and activate my FREE benefits -- immediately.

More great gifts and benefits to come.

_____

NAME (please print)

_____

ADDRESS   APT. NO

_____

CITY   STATE   ZIP/POSTAL CODE

PROOF OF PURCHASE

**NO CLUB!
NO COMMITMENT!**
*Just one purchase brings
you great Free Gifts and
Benefits!*

Please allow 6-8 weeks for delivery. Quantities are limited. We reserve the right to
substitute items. Enroll before October 31, 1995 and receive one full year of benefits.

Name of store where this book was purchased_____

Date of purchase_____

Type of store:

    ☐ Bookstore   ☐ Supermarket   ☐ Drugstore

    ☐ Dept. or discount store (e.g. K-Mart or Walmart)

    ☐ Other (specify)_____

Which Harlequin or Silhouette series do you usually read?

_____

Complete and mail with one Proof of Purchase and store receipt to:

U.S.: *PAGES & PRIVILEGES™*, P.O. Box 1960, Danbury, CT 06813-1960

Canada: *PAGES & PRIVILEGES™*, 49-6A The Donway West, P.O. 813,
       North York, ON M3C 2E8

SD-PP5B

"Is This Part Of The Cure?"

Kynan asked, his voice huskier than usual as Jenna lightly trailed her hand over his chest as if looking for other wounds.

Maybe touching him would be a cure, she thought dreamily. A cure for her inexplicable fascination with his body.

"I'm looking for other scratches," she said, careful to avoid touching the crystal device hanging over his heart.

"Actually, I think my scratch needs more than just an ointment."

"What does it need?"

"Psychological reinforcement. The human body heals far more quickly when the mind is relaxed."

Feeling greatly daring, Jenna trailed a fingertip along his jawline. "And what exactly would it take to relax your mind?"

Dear Reader,

Are you looking for books that are fresh, sexy, and wonderfully romantic? Then look no more, because you've got one of them in your hands right now! Silhouette Desire, where man meets woman...and love is the result.

When you enter the world of Silhouette Desire, you travel to places where the hero is passionate...ready to do *anything* to capture the eternal affections of the heroine. He's a guy you can't help but fall a little in love with yourself...just as the heroine does. And the heroine—whether she's a full-time mom or full-time career woman—is someone you can relate to!

And in Silhouette Desire you'll find some of romance fiction's finest writers. This month alone we have Dixie Browning, Lucy Gordon, BJ James, Susan Crosby, Judith McWilliams and Ryanne Corey. And where else, but in Silhouette Desire, will you find the *Man of the Month* or a bold, sensuous new miniseries such as MEN OF THE BLACK WATCH?

Silhouette Desire is simply *the* best in romance...this month and every month! So, enjoy....

Sincerely,

Lucia Macro
Senior Editor

Please address questions and book requests to:
Silhouette Reader Service
U.S.: 3010 Walden Ave., P.O. Box 1325, Buffalo, NY 14269
Canadian: P.O. Box 609, Fort Erie, Ont. L2A 5X3

JUDITH McWILLIAMS
THE MAN FROM ATLANTIS

SILHOUETTE *Desire*

Published by Silhouette Books

America's Publisher of Contemporary Romance

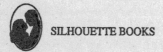

SILHOUETTE BOOKS

ISBN 0-373-05954-X

THE MAN FROM ATLANTIS

Copyright © 1995 by Judith McWilliams

This edition published by arrangement with Harlequin Books S.A.

® and TM are trademarks of Harlequin Books S.A., used under license.
Trademarks indicated with ® are registered in the United States Patent
and Trademark Office, the Canadian Trade Marks Office and in other
countries.

Printed in U.S.A.

JUDITH McWILLIAMS

began to enjoy romances while in search of the proverbial "happily ever afters." But she always found herself rewriting the endings, and eventually the beginnings, of the books she read. Then her husband finally suggested that she write novels of her own, and she's been doing so ever since. An ex-teacher with four children, Judith has traveled the country extensively with her husband and has been greatly influenced by those experiences. But while not tending the garden or caring for family, Judith does what she enjoys most—writing. She has also written under the name Charlotte Hines.

One

Jenna Farron instinctively froze as the ominous sound of a rattle echoed through the still, desert air. A chill feathered over her hot skin. As she hastily scanned the barren, rocky ground below, she wondered what a rattlesnake was doing out in the open. Normally, they had better sense than to subject their delicate bodies to the blistering heat of a July afternoon.

Jenna's stomach did a sudden flip-flop as she caught a flash of movement about twenty feet down the slope of the hill. She had been told that diamondback rattlers commonly grew to more than six feet, but knowing that intellectually and finding herself only a few yards from ten feet of slithering death, was quite another matter.

Blind fear engulfed her as the snake lifted its head and stared directly at her. She tried to comfort herself with the fact that there was a snake-bite kit back in her truck, not more than a mile away. And, if for some reason she couldn't reach the truck, she could always call for help. She touched the cellular phone strapped to her waistband like a talisman. She might be alone, but she was far from helpless.

She forced herself to remain motionless as the rattler suddenly slithered away, disappearing behind a large boulder.

Jenna let her breath out on a long, relieved sigh. The things they didn't tell you when you were studying to be an archaeologist, she thought ruefully as she pulled her hat off and ran her trembling fingers through short black hair, leaving behind yellowish dust streaks.

Turning to her left, away from the direction the rattler had gone, Jenna lost her balance on a loose piece of shale and began to slide down the side of the hill in a cascade of rocks and dirt. Frantically, she struggled to grab something, anything, to slow her descent. About three-quarters of the way down the steep incline, she managed to catch hold of a shrub, bringing herself to a sudden stop.

Looking down, her eyes narrowed as she caught a glimpse of blue in the rocks near the base of the hill.

A vein of turquoise? She awkwardly scrambled down the rest of the way to the thin line of blue. *No, not turquoise,* she realized. The color wasn't quite right, and the stone was too smooth. In fact... Jenna felt a sudden surge of excitement. It looked worked!

Hurriedly yanking her rock hammer out of her belt, she hunched down beside the blue stone and began to carefully chip away at the loose rocks around it. Working with as much speed as she could muster in the stifling heat, she swept and scraped and tossed the rocks away until she'd uncovered a piece of the bluish substance almost as tall as she was and about four feet wide.

Gingerly she ran her hand over the slick surface, pausing when she discovered a series of depressions. Flexing her fingers slightly, she stretched them to fit the indentations and then watched in disbelief as, with a rasping, creaking sound, the surface split and one side slowly rolled to the left.

Filled with a confusing mixture of excitement and fear, Jenna slowly counted to one hundred. When nothing else happened, she unhooked her halogen flashlight from her equipment belt and aimed the beam into the yawning blackness of the opening. The space inside appeared huge. *A cave?* she wondered.

She shone the light on the ground inside. It wasn't entirely natural, she realized, but paved with the same blue, marblelike material that had sealed the opening. Someone with a high degree of technology at their command had either built this or modified it. But who? Certainly not the prehistoric Indians she was investigating.

Unable to resist the lure, Jenna cautiously entered and swung her light around the chamber. The pale yellow beam arced to her right, over a box about seven feet long and three feet wide. It looked like...a coffin. A quiver of foreboding danced over her skin, raising goose bumps. Nervously she widened the arc of her flashlight, frustrated by her poor vision.

Jenna slowly approached the box. Standing on tiptoe, she awkwardly leaned over and peered through the crystal-clear lid. Her breath escaped in a disbelieving whoosh and her eyes widened incredulously. The sound of her own raspy breathing whistling through her open mouth finally penetrated her sense of shock. She blinked, closed her mouth and took a deep, sustaining breath. And then a second, when one wasn't enough.

"It's just a man," she assured herself aloud, focusing her flashlight on leanly chiseled features, and shortly cut, golden-yellow hair that reminded her of the first spring daffodils. His eyes were closed, but for some inexplicable reason Jenna was certain they were blue.

Had been blue, Jenna corrected herself. A powerful wave of loss slammed through her, leaving her feeling totally bereft. As if she'd just lost something of infinite value.

"Stop it," she ordered herself. "You aren't some impressionable primitive to be thrown off-balance by a..."

A what? Jenna wondered in confusion. What was this place? Who had built it, and how had they managed to preserve the man so perfectly? So very perfectly. Her eyes traced along the powerful thrust of his clean-shaven jaw, down the length of his neck to the broad expanse of his chest and lingered on the mat of golden curls with just the faintest tinge of red in them. Like antique gold jewelry, she thought fancifully. Her fingers tingled with an urge to touch it. To explore its texture. She clenched her hands into fists to dispel the compulsion and continued her inspection.

Following the trail of his body hair as it arrowed down his flat belly, she caught her breath as a surge of some unexpected emotion flooded her, momentarily short-circuiting her thought processes.

The very force of the reaction set off alarm bells deep in her mind. It was totally unlike her, and it made her very uneasy. She'd never been overly impressed by a man's physical attributes. She'd learned long ago that a beautiful body did not necessarily translate into a beautiful personality. Or, for that matter, even an adequate one. All too often, she'd found that very handsome, very well-built men seemed to feel that the rules of normal society didn't apply to them; that they had a right to take whatever and whomever they wanted.

So why her intense reaction to this man's physical perfection? Jenna's eyes moved back up his body, their progress slow like the turgid flow of dripping honey. Her eyelids drooped slightly under the weight of the heavy, languid emotions whirling through her. She tilted her head to one side, and studied the man with a concentration normally reserved for beloved artifacts.

Jenna blinked as she caught a reflected glint of light from her flashlight and realized the man wasn't entirely naked. Something gleamed around his neck. Leaning forward, she tried to see what it was but her breath fogged the cool surface of the lid, blurring her sight.

Impatiently, Jenna used the edge of her T-shirt to rub it dry and looked again. The thin golden chain was at first glance hard to distinguish from his body hair. Suspended from it was a small crystal ornament of some sort. She felt a flash of unease when, no matter how hard she tried, she couldn't quite make out its shape. It seemed to waver and shift as she stared at it.

Finally she gave up and looked back at the man's face. Despite the fact that he was absolutely still, her instinctive feeling was that he was not dead. But how could he be alive? The box was clearly sealed. Even if he'd been alive when he'd been entombed, he'd have long since suffocated.

Jenna carefully circled the box, studying it. The surface of the surrounding floor was smooth and unbroken. There were no pipes or tubes or anything that might serve to carry oxygen to the box's inhabitant. But despite the evidence of her eyes and the logic of her science, she couldn't quite shake her belief that the man was alive.

Jenna shone her pitifully inadequate light toward the wall behind the box. A large machine stood there. Resisting the impulse to look at the man again, she had almost reached the immense machine when she tripped over something on the floor and pitched forward, dropping the flashlight as she went. Instinctively, her hands thrust out to break her fall as she landed against the machine. Dozens of tiny buttons and levers pressed into her abused skin before she recovered enough to jerk backward. A high-pitched whine rolled over her head and echoed through the chamber and Jenna watched in dismay as more and more lights winked into existence down the machine's vast length.

Shifting from one foot to the other, Jenna frantically tried to undo whatever it was she'd inadvertently done, but it was difficult to think over the rapid beating of her heart. *Get out!* The order finally surfaced through her muddled thoughts.

She turned to run and then froze in horror as she realized the door was no longer open. She glanced over her shoulder at the machine's flickering lights. Had she closed the door herself when she'd hit the machine? Or had the machine closed it? To trap her?

Fear of being buried alive in the darkness swamped her common sense, and she sprinted toward the closed door, which shimmered with subdued light. Frantically she searched for the handhold that had originally opened the door, but found only smooth stone.

Finally conceding the futility of her actions, Jenna leaned her forehead against the cool surface and forced herself to think.

"You are trapped in an underground room." She stated her problem aloud, taking comfort from the sound of a human voice, even her own. "But not permanently," she assured herself. "You have options."

Her panic began to subside as she realized the chamber was now lit by a dim light that allowed her to make out banks of machines stretching off into the distance. She looked up but couldn't see the top of the chamber. Nor could she see where the diffused light was coming from. All she could see was that the light was definitely growing stronger by the minute.

Her momentary sense of relief was abruptly shattered when an odd, grating sound echoed through the funereal silence. The hair on the back of her neck lifted as she suddenly realized what the sound was. The lid of the box was opening!

Jenna swallowed against the metallic taste of fear that filled her mouth. Her heart rate accelerated, the beats coming so fast they merged one into another as the lid overbalanced and tumbled to the ground with a dull, muffled thud. As if the floor itself had somehow absorbed the sound.

A sharp, acrid odor polluted the air. It irritated Jenna's nose and made her eyes water. She rubbed the back of her hand across her eyelids, leaving dirt smears. Pulling a hammer out of her equipment belt and holding it in front like a weapon, Jenna waited, her nerves vibrating with tension. Just when she was beginning to think that nothing else was going to happen, a faint sound drifted to her.

Jenna froze, straining to hear. Silence. After what seemed like forever, she heard it again. A little louder this time. It was a groan. A very real, human groan. As if the man were in pain. Jenna gulped. In order to feel pain, he'd have to be alive; and he certainly hadn't seemed alive when she'd studied him.

Fear coated her skin with a cold sweat and she shivered, trying to think. She couldn't seem to get beyond the pain-filled sound the man had made. She felt a jab of guilt. She was the one who'd started the machine that had brought him back to consciousness. That she hadn't meant to do it was no excuse. The fact remained that she was the one responsible for his pain.

Shoving the hammer back into her belt, Jenna crept across the floor toward the box, stopping when she got close enough to catch a glimpse of movement from inside. Mesmerized, she watched the man's head appear above the side. His eyes were still closed, the muscles in his jaw were corded, and his lips were tightly compressed.

Tentatively, clumsily, the man levered himself up until Jenna had a clear view of his chest. She stared at the broad expanse, watching the way his labored breathing was forcing air into his rib cage. A tiny pulse beat frantically at the base of his throat, and she took an impulsive step forward, wanting to help.

The sound of her movement seemed to penetrate his stupor, and his head slowly turned toward her. Jenna held her ground with an effort. She assured herself that this man wasn't a threat to her. He was obviously physically incapable of harming anyone.

Jenna blinked as his eyelids lifted and he stared blankly at her with brilliant greenish-blue eyes. She'd never seen a color quite like them before. Not even among her friends who wore tinted contacts.

The man raised a shaking hand and rubbed his forehead as if trying to clear his thoughts. He stared at her for a long moment and then opened his mouth.

The deeply melodic, slightly muffled sound of his voice rolled warmly over her taut nerves, and Jenna unconsciously relaxed even though she didn't have the vaguest idea what he'd said.

"I'm sorry. I didn't quite catch that." She inched closer, drawn by his confused, lost expression.

He shook his head slightly, and his eyes widened as if the gesture had cost him dearly. With a visible effort, he dragged himself to his knees and stumbled out onto the floor.

He was taller than he'd appeared to be when lying down, Jenna realized. At least six-two, maybe more. And he was much broader, too.

"I'm Jenna Farron." She pointed to herself. "And you're..." She pointed at him. Apparently he hadn't seen the same Tarzan movies, because he ignored her. Instead, he stared around the chamber in a bemused fashion as if he wasn't quite sure where he was or how he'd gotten there. Stepping forward, he blindly clutched for the edge of the box as his legs buckled.

Jenna reacted instinctively. Her arms closed around his rib cage, and she braced his limp body against hers. Her cheek, pressed into his chest, was tickled by his crisp body hair. But the sensation didn't make her want to laugh. It made her feel warm. Warm and heavy and languid. And that made her feel nervous.

"Are you all right?" she mumbled against his icy skin and then winced at the inanity of the question. A three-year-old could see he wasn't all right.

He took a deep breath, and Jenna felt his muscles tense as he pulled away from her with an obvious effort. Staggering slightly, he stumbled toward the huge machine Jenna had fallen against. For a long moment, he simply leaned against it, his ragged breathing the only sound in the still air.

Warily Jenna watched him as he began to push buttons. What had she accidentally stumbled across? Who was he? Or maybe the question she should be asking was *what* was he? Her eyes narrowed thoughtfully. Could he be from space?

She weighed the fantastic thought. Maybe this complex had been built by a spaceship exploring earth. Maybe he had accidentally been stranded here and had put himself into some kind of protective sleep. Sleep that she'd disturbed when she'd fallen against the machine.

Jenna shifted uncertainly. It was an intriguing thought, but even she, who didn't know a great deal about biology, did know the odds were against a spaceman looking like an artistic representation of an early Greek god. Different environments produced different beings, and this guy looked as though he'd come straight from Central Casting.

Jenna frowned and looked around the room again. Could this be some kind of movie set? Or an elaborate practical joke? Or maybe something to do with a biosphere experiment?

Deciding that she had nothing to lose by asking, she cleared her throat and said, "Um, excuse me? But who are you?"

He turned, gave her a long, thoughtful look and then headed toward the far end of the room. Stopping about halfway down a row of cabinets, he placed the flat of his hand against the black surface and a door silently slid open.

Was that some kind of lock set to his palm print? Jenna wondered. Or to anyone's? A flicker of excitement dislodged some of her apprehension. If she could open those doors, what might she find behind them?

For that matter, what had he found? She watched as he took out a box about six inches square. It was built of some dark substance and, other than a few knobs on the top, was smooth.

He carried it over and set it down in front of her.

Jenna jumped as he pushed one of the knobs, and the box gave off a screech.

"I am Kynan of the House of Phelan," he said, and the box somehow reissued his voice in English.

Jenna stared at it in shock. "'Star Trek,' as I live and breathe," she muttered.

"No, Kynan," he repeated impatiently. "What happened?"

"I accidentally woke you up. What are you doing here and why were you in that box? And why weren't you breathing?"

"One does not breathe in suspended animation."

Jenna blinked uncertainly. Suspended animation would neatly explain it. At least it would if science had the capabilities to put someone in suspended animation. Which it didn't. So it followed that Kynan wasn't from Earth. Could her original guess really have been right? Could he be from space?

"Would you mind telling me why you were hiding out here in suspended animation?" she asked.

"I was waiting for the meteorites to impact. I just—" He was interrupted by a plucking noise from the machine. It was so high-pitched, it made Jenna's one filling ache.

Kynan hurried back to the console and pushed a button.

Jenna blinked in surprise as a crystal-clear picture suddenly formed on the screen above the console. Wincing, she glanced away from the sight of bloody corpses lying in a street.

"What!" Kynan muttered, paling visibly as he stared at the screen.

Jenna shuddered, sharing his sense of appalled horror.

"Those children..." He gestured with a shaking finger at one particularly grisly shot. "They appear to be dead."

Kynan turned and looked at her. All the color had leeched out of his face and his brilliant eyes were dimmed with a shocked, lost expression.

Jenna felt her heart twist in sympathy. She wanted to throw her arms around him and comfort him, but her innate sense of shyness held her immobile.

"I think you'd better sit down before you fall down," she urged him, worried by his increasing paleness.

Kynan looked down his slightly oversize nose at her. "I am not going to fall down," he announced and then promptly collapsed into a heap on the floor like a balloon that had suddenly sprung a leak.

Anxiously, Jenna studied him. It was distinctly chilly in here and probably would get worse before morning. Shivering, she wrapped her arms around her chest. She was cold and she had clothes on. Kynan must be freezing.

Hoping there might be something she could use to cover him, she hurried to the cabinets at the far end of the room. But repeated attempts to open them with her hand, as she'd seen Kynan do, failed. Either the locks were set to his handprint or there was some trick she didn't know. Probably the latter, she thought in frustration. There seemed to be so much about this situation that she didn't know.

She returned to Kynan and sat down beside him, studying the waxy color of his skin nervously. He was obviously extremely weak, and if he were to become chilled...

She gently shook his shoulder. His skin felt firm and supple and very cold beneath her fingers. She shook harder, trying to wake him. He didn't move.

Jenna took a deep breath, trying to think—something she seemed to be having a great deal of trouble doing. One fact finally surfaced through her confusion. Kynan needed to be kept warm and, since she was the only warm thing in this place, it was up to her to do what she could. Squelching her instinctive fear of being rebuffed, Jenna scooted closer to him, snuggling against his chest.

The combined warmth of their bodies began to seep into her muscles, and she drifted off to sleep.

When she awoke it was to find Kynan standing in front of the console screen, studying a picture of what appeared to be the outside landscape. His face was taut, with deep lines etched into either side of his mouth.

"Good morning," she offered tentatively.

He turned and stared blankly at her as if he'd never seen her before.

"I definitely need to work on creating a better first impression," she muttered.

"So do I, but I am over ten thousand years too late. We must have taken a direct hit. Everything is gone," he said bluntly. "My people. Atlantis—"

"Atlantis is just a myth," Jenna objected.

"Like hell it is! I am from Atlantis."

"Not from space?" Jenna suddenly realized that he was speaking English. She looked around for the translating device, but it was no longer there. How could he be speaking English?

"I have never been any farther in space than a holiday cruise to the outer planets, and I found it a total waste of time."

Jenna eyed him thoughtfully, wondering whether or not to believe him. Holiday cruises to the outer planets sounded far-fetched, but then this whole thing was pretty far-fetched.

"You said something about meteorites?" Jenna remembered.

"We discovered that a stream of meteorites was headed toward Earth," he said slowly, as if reluctant to remember. "One faction of the government felt that Earth would be destroyed, and they elected to put all their efforts into building a space fleet to escape the solar system. While the rest of us..." He ran his shaking fingers through his hair. "We thought the meteorites would merely cause heavy flooding for a few years and then recede."

"I don't know if that's what happened, but I can tell you that virtually every culture on Earth has a great flood as part of its oral tradition," she told him. "But the only mention of Atlantis is by Plato in *Timaeus* and again in *Critias* and that's just legend. Certainly there's never been any proof. Not even a fragment of an artifact."

"Tell me, how would your culture fare if all your cities were suddenly washed away?" he demanded.

"We'd probably descend into barbarism rather quickly," Jenna conceded.

A pained expression flittered across his face. "From what I have seen so far, you have not climbed out of it yet."

Jenna opened her mouth and then closed it. There was just enough truth in what he was saying that she couldn't effectively deny it. Even her own government—which was supposed to be answerable to the people—played by its own set of rules when it was expedient.

She studied Kynan speculatively. He didn't look very good. Although, if he were telling the truth and he really had just been rousted out of a state of suspended animation after ten thousand years to find that everyone and everything he knew was long gone, then he was actually doing rather well. Under the circumstances.

Uncertainly she chewed on her lower lip. She didn't know what to believe. This whole fantastic complex, as well as Kynan's obvious physical distress, tended to support his story. One thing she knew for certain was that if he really was a refugee from Atlantis, he was the biggest archaeological find of all time. Everyone from the supermarket tabloids to the CIA would be clamoring to talk to him.

But he was more than just a potential source of historical information, she thought protectively. Kynan was a man. A thinking, feeling man. She stared at the corded muscles in his jaw. Corded, she suspected, by the effort he was making to control his fear and uncertainty. Whatever the truth, Kynan needed time and space to adjust.

Something the authorities wouldn't give him, Jenna conceded, having no illusions about her society's shortcomings. But she could give Kynan a safe sanctuary while he regained his strength and came to grips with what had happened to him—whatever that was.

A sense of rightness flowed soothingly through her tired mind. She would take Kynan home with her and give him a chance to get his bearings without any outside pressure. And if—incredible as it seemed—it turned out he actually was from Atlantis, maybe he'd be willing to talk to her about his life there. Anticipation sent a hectic flush across her cheeks.

"How did you learn to speak English in a matter of hours?" Jenna homed in on the one part of his story that bothered her the most.

"I tapped into the computer records at the library of some university, fed that information into the hypolearners and used it."

"Of course, a 'hypolearner.' How handy." She gave up. He commanded machines she couldn't understand, and perhaps a hypolearner—whatever that was—was just one more.

"I don't know about you, but I want coffee, breakfast and a hot shower," she said.

Kynan looked around the cavern in a slightly dazed manner, as if the idea of sustenance had never occurred to him. Then he looked up at the screen showing a view of the inhospitable desert outside. "That does seem to present a problem," he muttered.

"It doesn't have to," Jenna said carefully. "I have a truck not too far from here. I could take you back to my house where you could rest and regain your strength."

Kynan tilted his head to one side and stared at her. His brilliant blue-green eyes seemed to glitter with the force of his thoughts.

The skin on Jenna's face tightened under the impact of his gaze, which felt as if it were a live entity, actually touching her. It made her uncomfortable and excited in a way that was new to her, and she wasn't sure she liked it.

"I do have a problem, but are you part of the solution?" he murmured, as if thinking aloud.

Jenna held her breath, refusing to admit even to herself just how much she wanted him to come with her.

He slowly walked toward her, stopping two feet away, with his hands held out, palms up. The gesture was unmistakable. He wanted her to place her hands against his. As a symbol of peace? Agreement? She didn't know.

Jenna rubbed her palms down over her jeans to wipe away the grime and then placed her hands on his. His skin felt warm. Warm and faintly callused as if he were used to hard work. She glanced up into his eyes. If he really had come from Atlantis, what had his role there been?

Her train of thought was abruptly derailed as a powerful wave of... something flooded her, catching her completely off guard. Brilliant, scintillating sparks of silvery light darted through her mind, picking at her thoughts. Thoroughly shaken, she reacted instinctively, jerking backward.

"What did you do?" she demanded.

Kynan stared at her, weighing his answer. What should he tell her? The truth? She did not appear to have the background to understand even the simple thought scan he'd attempted to do. To her, it had been totally unknown. Something threatening. But he had learned two things before she'd broken contact. Jenna Farron might be leery of both him and his story, but she was not inimical toward him.

Nor did she share the bloodthirsty traits of her contemporaries on the broadcast waves he had been monitoring.

He studied her pale features, his eyes lingering on the dark shadows under her black eyes.

She was right. He did need food and shelter. He probed the depth of the tiredness that dragged at him and found it boundless. He'd taken the restorative that had been left for him, but he needed to sleep while it worked. And where could he find a safe haven from the insanity that raged outside?

A jagged shard of grief slashed at his composure. With a monumental effort, he pushed it to the back of his mind. This wasn't the time to dwell on what he'd lost. This was the time to focus on what he could salvage. Once he'd recovered physically and mentally, he could make contact with his compatriots who had left Earth in the spaceships before the impact. They could rescue him from this madhouse. The thought steadied him.

Making up his mind, he said, "All right, I'll go with you."

"Open the door and let me out." Jenna tried to sound matter-of-fact when inside she was a seething mass of excitement. "I'll get the truck and drive it as close to here as I can."

"Yes, the door," Kynan repeated, making a tremendous effort to fight off the exhaustion fogging his mind. He needed to stay alert long enough to choose what he wanted to take with him from the cave. Clumsily he reached for the proper button and pushed it. The door opened with a rasping sound.

An overwhelming sense of relief flooded Jenna at the sight of the bright morning sunlight outside. She took an instinctive step toward it and then turned back to Kynan.

"Will you be all right?" she asked, not wanting to leave him alone, but seeing no alternative. He didn't look strong enough to walk the distance to the truck.

She watched in fascination as his lips lifted in a wry grin that unexpectedly tugged at her heart.

"In a physical or a philosophical sense?" he asked.

Jenna chuckled, feeling better about him. "Don't move. I'll be right back."

She raced out the door, intent on getting Kynan home as soon as possible. His unexpected invasion of her mind—which he hadn't bothered to explain, she suddenly realized—had finally convinced her that Kynan was exactly what he said he was. A displaced citizen of Atlantis. Which no doubt accounted for her uncharacteristic reaction to him. She could only hope that once she got him away from that strange installation and into some clothes, she'd be able to view him with more normal detachment. If not...if her compulsive attraction to him grew...

It won't, she assured herself as she scrambled up the side of the hill. No man had been able to distract her from her work yet, and a ten-thousand-year-old nude hunk with strange powers would not be the first.

Two
___

Jenna surreptitiously studied Kynan as she waited for the streetlight to change. The bright sunlight seemed to emphasize the grayish cast of his skin, and there were deeply carved lines around his tightly compressed lips. Maybe she was doing the wrong thing by taking him home with her, she thought in a burst of panic. Maybe she should be more concerned with his physical health than with his mental health.

"How are you feeling?" she asked him.

"How do you think I am feeling! I have just been jerked out of a state of suspended animation to find that I am trapped in an insane asylum and—"

"There's no reason to get testy," she said soothingly. "Would you prefer to still be back there sleeping your life away?"

Kynan stared moodily out the window, his gaze lingering on the scraps of litter on the side of the city street. "Maybe I am still asleep," he muttered. "Maybe this is all just a nightmare caused by the suspended animation. We really did not know very much about the process. If the situation had not been so desperate, we would never have used it on people without years more testing. Maybe you are not real. Maybe this whole thing—'' he waved his arms toward the scene outside, and the blanket slipped to his waist ''—is just a dream.''

''You let anyone see you running around without any clothes on and your dream is going to develop some awkward sequences,'' Jenna warned him.

''Probably not a dream. You are much too positive to be an illusion.'' He leaned back against the headrest and closed his eyes.

Too positive? Jenna examined his description and, with an inward sigh of regret, decided he probably didn't mean it as a compliment. In her experience men didn't like positive women, but instead felt threatened by them.

She pressed down on the accelerator, eager to get home and put Kynan to bed where he could sleep and, hopefully, recuperate. If he didn't . . . She'd cross that bridge when she got to it.

Five minutes later, Jenna turned into the driveway of the tiny house she'd rented for the summer. Fumbling in the glove compartment for the automatic garage-door opener, she caught sight of her elderly neighbor waving at her from across the street.

Jenna finally located the opener and activated it, mentally urging the slow-moving garage door to hurry as she pretended not to notice Mrs. Coltrain's gestures. While Jenna didn't want to snub the old woman, she wanted even less to try explaining the strange man, wrapped in a blanket and nothing else, sitting beside her.

The garage door finally opened, and Jenna pulled inside, hastily closing the door behind her.

Her shoulders sagged in relief as she switched off the truck's engine. Now, to get Kynan out of the garage and into...where? The question suddenly occurred to her. Where was she going to put him? Her tiny house had one small bedroom and an oversize broom closet the rental agent had optimistically called a maid's room—exactly big enough to contain a single bed and nothing else. In fact, there was only twelve inches of floor space around the bed. She could just manage to squeeze through the door.

Her eyes slowly swept down Kynan's long, muscular length. He'd never fit through that narrow opening. Which left the double bed in the bedroom for him and the lumpy mattress in the maid's room for her. Ah, well, she mentally shrugged, she'd slept in far more primitive conditions while out in the field on archaeological digs.

Kynan opened his eyes and stared at her in obvious confusion. His pupils were enormous black pools with only a thin rim of color around the edges. He lifted his head as if the effort was almost more than he could manage and slowly looked around the inside of her garage.

"Where are we?" he asked.

"My home. At least, my home for the summer. Wait a minute," she said as he fumbled with the door handle. "I'll help you."

"You can help by giving me some assistance with my equipment." He gestured toward the bed of the truck, piled high with various containers he'd insisted on taking from the bunker despite her attempts to convince him that they should return for them later.

"Kynan," she began, "you need—"

"To unpack my equipment." The words escaped from between his clenched teeth.

Jenna gave up, recognizing a lost cause when she saw it. He wasn't open to reason at the moment. He was operating on instinct, and instinct was telling him to take care of the most important things he had left. Those boxes. She felt a flash of curiosity as to what might be in them.

"I'll help. In fact, I'll do the whole thing," she said. "You can supervise."

"You can not," he said.

"Of course I can. I loaded half of them in the first place."

"And you can unload that half, but the others are too heavy for you."

"Sure. Not only do you look like death warmed over, but your coordination is shot. And you expect me to believe that you're stronger than I am, right now?"

"It is not a matter of muscles," he said. "It is a matter of the unit being personalized to my wavelength."

Jenna stared at him in confusion. "The words are English, but they don't make any sense, taken as a whole."

"You cannot understand me because your language is inadequate to express what I'm trying to say," he said in frustration. "What I meant was my antigravity device only operates on my brain-wave patterns. And negating the effects of gravity was what allowed me to carry all these boxes from the cave to your truck."

Jenna blinked. "Antigravity device?"

"Look." Kynan stepped out of the truck, forgetting the blanket.

Jenna looked and then wished she hadn't. She found it very difficult to concentrate on what he was saying when she focused on how he looked.

He turned and opened his hand, showing her a small, green crystalline box about three inches long and an inch thick. Jenna recognized it as having been sitting on top of each pile of boxes Kynan had carried. She assumed he had kept it so close because it was too important to be allowed out of his sight.

Kynan walked around to the back of the truck, Jenna right behind him, and pointed to one of the containers he'd loaded. It was about the size of a shoe box. "Try to lift that," he said.

Jenna reached into the truck bed and grabbed the container with one hand. It didn't move. She tried with both hands. It wouldn't budge. Whatever was in there was incredibly heavy. Refusing to give up, she scrambled into the truck to get better leverage. All she could manage to do was shift the box a few inches along the floor. "I can't lift it," she finally conceded.

"Now watch." He placed the small device on top of the box and the box immediately floated into the air.

Jenna sucked in her breath in sudden excitement. "How big an object does that work on?" she demanded.

"Not too big. Certainly nothing bigger than your vehicle. This unit was meant to be used around the lab for moving small items."

Jenna eyed the device longingly. One of those things would be invaluable to an archaeologist in the field. What else had Kynan's Atlantis had? Anticipation curled through her at the thought, but she reined in her enthusiasm with an effort. Kynan was in no condition to be bombarded with questions. He needed to rest. And before he was willing to rest, he was determined to unpack his things.

Jenna grabbed a stack of boxes she had loaded earlier. In her haste, the top carton overbalanced and fell back into the truck on top of her sack of supplies.

Jenna winced at the sound of shattering glass.

Kynan's head jerked up. "What was that?"

"Don't worry. It wasn't your stuff," she assured him. She gently moved the carton and upended the sack, watching as a stream of white powder mixed with shards of brown glass poured out.

"I just broke my jar of coffee creamer." Jenna carefully picked up the pieces of glass and dropped them back into the empty sack. "I'll sweep this up later."

But despite her efforts to hurry and Kynan's use of the antigravity device, it took almost twenty minutes for them to finish. An interminably frustrating twenty minutes during which Jenna watched as what little strength Kynan had left drained away. Finally he unloaded the last container and then sagged limply against the side of her dusty truck.

"Sorry," he muttered, his voice a thin thread of sound. "I seem to be a little tired."

"If this is your definition of a little, I hope I never see what you consider a lot," Jenna said, concern sharpening her voice. She grabbed for him as he stumbled.

Kynan fell against her, almost knocking her over. Jenna locked her muscles and, putting her arms around his waist, supported him as they made their wavering way into the house. The crisp hair on his chest scraped across her arm, sending shivers of awareness skittering along her nerve endings.

Jenna ran her tongue over her dry lips, telling herself that her reaction was entirely inappropriate. She should be thinking of how to help Kynan get well, not of how much she wanted to touch him. The only problem was that while her mind was willing to concede these points, her body didn't seem to care. It reacted to him on a level that owed nothing to intellect. It was all instinct. An instinct she hadn't even realized she possessed until now.

Of course, she was reacting to him in an uncharacteristic manner, she rationalized. He was the first Atlantean she'd ever run across. She was allowed a few aberrations from her normal mode of behavior. Her grip tightened as he stumbled slightly.

"So sorry." His voice was a long drawn-out sigh that wafted over her cheek, warming her skin. "I can't seem to make my muscles do what I tell them. All I need is a rest...."

There was a faintly panicky note underlying his words that Jenna responded to automatically. "You'll be fine in a few days," she reassured him, praying it was true. "We'll pop you in bed, and you can sleep for as long as you need."

She pushed open the door to her bedroom with her foot, grateful for the room's small dimensions. It was only a matter of a few feet from the door to the double bed.

Kynan collapsed on it, and his eyes closed.

"Don't go to sleep yet," she said.

"Why not?" His voice sounded faint and far away.

"Because you're a couple thousand years too late for Rome."

Kynan opened one eye and peered up at her. "Rome? I find the reference meaningless."

"Rome was an ancient civilization where the men wore pieces of cloth called togas similar to that blanket I gave you to wear."

"I have never been the slightest interested in the fashions of any culture."

"I have to get you some clothes," she insisted.

He stared at her for a long moment as if he were having trouble coordinating his thoughts. "Yes," he finally agreed. "Camouflage. An excellent idea."

"But to do that, I need to know what size to buy, which means I have to measure you. Wait here while I get a tape measure," she ordered.

He chuckled weakly and the rueful sound tugged enticingly at her emotions. "I do not think I could move if my life depended on it, my dear Jenna. Go get your measuring device."

Jenna went. She found her sewing basket on the bed in the spare bedroom and rummaged through it, finding the tape measure under the embroidery floss. She rushed back to the bedroom, worried that he might have fallen asleep. To her relief, his eyes were still open, but unfocused.

"If you'll just sit up," she suggested, trying not to let her eyes stray down the length of his body.

"Be quick," he muttered as he used his elbow to try to lever himself up. Jenna grabbed his arm and helped. His skin felt warm. Too warm? she worried with a quick look at

his face. There were two spots of color high on his cheekbones, and his eyes had a bright, febrile glitter to them.

Jenna hurriedly wrapped the tape measure around his
lean waist and then his chest, quickly memorizing the numbers.

"There." She tossed the measure onto the dresser. "Do
you want an electric razor or manual one?"

"Neither. I had my facial hair eradicated years ago."

"Oh." Jenna firmly squelched her desire to ask more
questions. "I'll go get something for you to wear after I have
breakfast, so if you should wake up and I'm not here, don't
worry.

"Do you want some breakfast before I go?" She suddenly remembered that he hadn't had a good square meal in
over ten thousand years.

A spasm of revulsion crossed his face. "No, I just want
to sleep." He closed his eyes.

Jenna stared down at him, watching as his breathing
slowed and developed an even cadence that lifted his rib
cage with soothing regularity.

He'd be all right, she told herself, to quiet her fears. He
just needed to sleep. And he had taken that liquid he'd called
a restorative. Kynan believed it would return him to normal. Of course, he'd also believed that fancy machine of his
would keep him asleep for only a few hundred years. The
disquieting thought suddenly surfaced.

"Don't borrow trouble," Jenna muttered as she went to
the closet and got a blanket. She carefully covered Kynan,
tucking the blanket around his shoulders. With the air-
conditioning running, it was chilly inside and he didn't need
a cold on top of all he'd been through.

Finally, after another ten minutes of watching Kynan
sleep, Jenna quietly rummaged through her bureau, extracted clean clothes, and headed toward the bathroom. She
felt dusty, grimy and full of sand. A quick shower would
take care of that problem.

Fifteen minutes later, clean and feeling a little more alert, she fixed herself a bowl of cereal and flipped on the television to watch the local news. She was listening absently when the broadcast suddenly took an ominous turn.

The announcer gave his television audience a condescending smirk and announced, "Now, for all you believers in visitors from the stars, we have a news flash for you."

Jenna paused, her spoon of cereal halfway to her mouth, and leaned toward the vapidly grinning newscaster. What did he mean? she wondered uneasily.

Unfortunately for her peace of mind, she wasn't left wondering for long.

The announcer's grin broadened. "This morning the station received a call from—" he glanced down at his notes "—a young man coming home late last night, who informs us that as he was crossing the desert about fifty miles northeast of El Paso he saw a series of blue lights shimmering on the horizon. According to our anonymous informant, the lights appeared and disappeared in a random pattern."

Jenna set her half-finished bowl of cereal down on the coffee table, no longer hungry. Fifty miles northeast of El Paso put the sighting near the cave where she'd found Kynan. Could what the man have seen somehow be connected to Kynan? She chewed on her lower lip as she tried to think. Kynan had operated that machine last night. Could the machine have been responsible for the bluish lights? Or could it simply be a coincidence? Could the anonymous caller have seen a natural phenomenon? There were certainly enough of them to see around here. The lights of Marfa had never been properly explained and people had been seeing them for hundreds of years.

"Unfortunately, our caller refused to leave his name," the newscaster continued. "Otherwise we could have asked him what kind of refreshment he'd been indulging in before he went home."

Jenna hit the Off button on the remote control and stared thoughtfully at the blank screen. After the distinctly patronizing manner of that newscaster, whoever had called in the original sighting would have to be a very determined individual to pursue what he'd seen. And she rather doubted the unknown informant was that determined or he would have given his name in the first place.

She relaxed slightly. Not only that, but the chamber where she'd found Kynan was located on private land. Private, fenced land. Judging from her own frustrating experience with Bob Lessing, who owned that land, he would not be agreeable to letting sightseers or anyone else, roam around disturbing his precious cattle.

In fact, Lessing repeatedly had turned down her requests to look for artifacts on his ranch. It was only after the president of her university had asked one of the Texas senators to intervene that Lessing had finally given Jenna permission to do some preliminary exploration. But even that grudging consent had been qualified with a long list of areas that were strictly off-limits to her.

No, she thought in satisfaction. Bob Lessing would never allow curiosity seekers on his land. And since Kynan was now here and not there to activate the machine again, there wouldn't be anything else to see.

Grabbing her purse, Jenna hurried out to the garage, wanting to get her shopping over with as soon as possible. As she backed the truck out, she caught sight of Mrs. Coltrain still working in her front garden across the street. Jenna watched in her rearview mirror as the old woman waved and started toward her. Knowing that Mrs. Coltrain would persist until she discovered who Kynan was, Jenna rolled down her window and waited.

"Good morning, Mrs. Coltrain," Jenna said. "Your Shasta daisies are looking great."

"Thank you, Jenna." Mrs. Coltrain's nose twitched eagerly as she glanced from the empty seat beside Jenna, and back toward the house. "Leaving your visitor all alone so soon after he arrived?"

"He's not exactly a visitor." Jenna scrambled for an excuse, wishing that she'd had the foresight to think of a cover story before she'd left. The problem was that she was tired. Her nap last night on the cave's stone floor had not left her at her best, either physically or mentally.

"He's a visiting professor who'll be teaching at my university this fall. From Sweden," Jenna added, in the hopes that a Scandinavian background would explain his blondness as well as any social or language mistakes he might make. "He had a few weeks free, and he wanted to see what I've discovered in my dig this summer."

Mrs. Coltrain nodded her snowy head. "Ah, that would explain why he looked so tired. You must have just picked him up at the airport?"

"Hmm, flights are so exhausting, aren't they? And he's been in rather uncertain health recently," Jenna added. "I left him taking a nap."

"Poor man," Mrs. Coltrain said sympathetically. "Well, our good desert air will have him back on his feet in no time, and it'll be so nice for you to have some company.

"I won't keep you since I know how hard you work." Mrs. Coltrain stepped back from the truck. "But you must allow me to invite you both for dinner."

"Dinner?" Jenna repeated weakly. Not only was there the problem of what Kynan might inadvertently say if she took him out in public, but she had no idea what he might eat. For all she knew, he could be used to some sort of exotic diet.

"I'll make Swedish meatballs." Mrs. Coltrain beamed at her.

"Lovely. I'll check with him and see about his schedule," Jenna said and then escaped before Mrs. Coltrain could manage to pin her down to a definite date.

Keeping Kynan hidden was not going to be an easy matter, she realized as she headed toward the mall. But the alternative of turning him over to a bunch of self-serving politicians in the government was unthinkable. Jenna felt a surge of protectiveness as she remembered the confused, panicked expression in Kynan's eyes when he'd first awoken. He needed time to adjust before he had to deal with the future and she was going to make sure he got it. Her lips firmed in an uncharacteristically militant expression.

"Colonel Macintosh to see Major Defton." The tall man announced his presence to the woman behind the desk.

"Good morning, Colonel. It's good to see you back," Claudia said, receiving a stony stare in exchange. Undaunted, she gave him a warm smile.

"The major is expecting you, sir." Claudia nodded to the door to her right. "Go down the corridor. Major Defton's office is the third door on the right."

"Thank you." Carrying his body with ramrod stiffness, Macintosh marched through the door, closing it behind him with a snap.

"Whew!" The woman who was filing letters on the other side of the room grimaced. "I always liked the strong silent type, but that one is carrying a good thing to extremes."

"I feel sorry for him," Claudia said. "He had a heart operation last month."

Linda blinked in surprise. "Him? He didn't look a day over forty."

"I don't think he is. I wonder why the major wants him?"

Macintosh was wondering the same thing as he slowly walked down the corridor toward Defton's office. He started to rub his chest, which ached, and then cursed under his breath when he realized what he was doing.

Stopping outside Defton's office, he carefully checked the front of his uniform. It was spotless. Taking a deep breath, he rapped sharply on the door and at the command to enter, did so.

Major Defton was seated behind a huge desk piled high with stacks of paper, newspapers, folders and what appeared to be assorted junk.

Macintosh eyed him thoughtfully. He didn't know much about Defton other than that he had something to do with security. Macintosh's curiosity about why he'd been summoned increased.

When the hospital had certified him as being fit for restricted duty, he'd hoped that he could make a positive contribution somewhere while he waited for his heart to heal, but so far his contributions had consisted of speaking to one garden club, a Brownie troop and a civic group. Unfortunately, the flowers had made him sneeze; the little girls he'd liked—in the abstract—but in reality he hadn't had the vaguest idea what one said to a bunch of six-year-olds; and the civic group had infuriated him with their narrow-minded view on the future of the military. Whatever this Major Defton wanted, it couldn't be any worse than the assignments he'd already drawn.

"Ah, Colonel, have a seat." Defton nodded toward the chair in front of his desk.

Macintosh gingerly sat down and willed Defton to hurry. The ache in his chest was escalating, and he needed to get to his quarters and take his medicine before it got any worse. He didn't want to do it in front of Defton. The major might mention it to someone and before he knew it, there would be gossip all over the base about how his angioplasty had failed.

"No doubt, you're wondering why I asked you to stop by," Defton began. "It was because you were recommended to me as intelligent, thorough and meticulous. And, more importantly, as a man who could keep his mouth shut. We need someone who's discreet to investigate something. Did you happen to catch the local news this morning?"

"Yes."

"Do you remember the part about the anonymous caller who claimed to have seen mysterious lights out in the desert last night?"

Macintosh felt his brief spurt of interest drain away. My God, he thought bitterly, had he been relegated to chasing flying-saucer sightings?

"I remember," he said tightly.

Defton gave him a shrewd glance. "But didn't believe it. Can't say as I do, either, but the fact is, something played holy hell with the base's radar last night."

"How?"

"We don't know how. If we knew how, we might know who. Engineering leans toward the 'unusual atmospheric conditions' theory, while the commander is pushing for a malfunction in the equipment."

"And you?" Macintosh asked.

Defton sighed and tugged absently on his earlobe. "I'm not sure what I believe. Natural phenomenon as an explanation is far too pat and the odds are against all the equipment malfunctioning at the same time.... To make matters worse, we have a complication by the name of Ed Winkler."

Macintosh frowned, not recognizing the name. "And he is?"

Defton snorted. "Ed Winkler is a local nut who firmly believes in flying saucers, and he has a positive genius for getting publicity. He's already had an interview with the paper. He's claiming that the lights the anonymous caller reported were caused by an alien spaceship crashing in the desert and that the army knows about it and is trying to hush up the affair.

"Unfortunately, flying saucer reports always capture the public imagination, and we've already had some calls demanding that we release information we don't have. The commander feels it's essential that we give the appearance of being very candid about the whole thing so as not to give the antimilitary groups any ammunition to use against us. That's why he suggested that you look into it. He's hoping that when we release a meticulously detailed investigation that doesn't find any evidence of extraterrestrials, Winkler will shut up."

"Maybe," Macintosh said doubtfully. From his experience, fanatics weren't open to either logic or reason.

"There's something else," Defton continued. "I checked with the local office of the FBI this morning to see if they knew anything about what happened last night. They said that as near as they can tell, those blue lights that were reported were either on or very near a ranch owned by a man named Lessing, who has strong ties to a Colombian drug lord.

"The FBI is sure that Lessing's using his ranch as a stopover for smuggling drugs from South America into the U.S. They just haven't been able to prove it yet."

Macintosh whistled. "Drug smuggling is a far more rational explanation for interrupted radar than little green men from Mars."

"A hell of a lot more dangerous, too," Defton warned. "The commander isn't asking you to tangle with a drug cartel. All he wants you to do is document in excruciatingly boring detail the fact that those mysterious lights weren't caused by flying saucers. If you do happen to stumble across anything pertaining to drug smuggling, he said to call the FBI and let them handle it."

Macintosh got to his feet. "I'll do my best, Major."

"Thanks, Colonel. I really appreciate your helping us out. If you need any assistance, Artie Bradshaw isn't very busy at the moment. Ask him."

Macintosh nodded noncommittally and left. Help? He grimaced. To do what? To corral all the spacemen bent on conquering the Earth? The way the world was going lately, he thought sourly, it might be weeks before anyone would even notice the Earth had been invaded.

Three

___

Jenna's head jerked up as she heard a muffled sound from her bedroom. Tossing aside the newspaper she'd been reading, she hurried down the short hallway to the closed bedroom door. After two seemingly interminable days, Kynan was finally stirring!

She pressed her ear against the flimsy bedroom door and listened. A feeling of jubilant anticipation surged through her as she heard a thud, followed by an irritable-sounding voice muttering what she was willing to bet were curses.

At last! Kynan was awake. Suddenly, for some reason she didn't quite understand but relished all the same, the world seemed in sharper focus. She scurried back into the living room and plopped down on the sofa, not wanting to be caught standing guard outside his door. She didn't want to do anything to upset him. At least, to upset him any further than he already was.

She glanced down at the morning paper and winced when

she saw the gruesome headline. Hurriedly she shoved it under the couch.

She took several deep breaths to calm the excited thumping of her heart and waited. She heard the sound of the shower running and then silence. A silence that stretched on and on. Impatiently, Jenna checked the time. It had been fifteen minutes since he'd turned off the shower. Could he have gone back to sleep? Her spirits plummeted at the thought.

Finally, just when she had resigned herself to waiting yet longer, the door to the bedroom opened and Kynan appeared. Avidly, Jenna studied him. He was wearing some of the clothes she'd bought, but they did little to camouflage his blatant masculinity. In fact, in some strange way, the jeans and denim shirt emphasized it, making her even more aware of him as a sensual being.

On a physical level, he looked much better than the last time she'd seen him awake. His stance was now straight and assured and the deeply carved lines beside his mouth were gone, as was the grayish cast to his skin. And his eyes... Jenna swallowed uncertainly as she found her gaze caught and held by his glittering blue-green eyes. If the eyes really were the windows of the soul, then Kynan's soul was filled with an incredible assortment of intriguing emotions she wanted to explore.

"Good morning," she said.

"Figuratively or literally?"

"Politely," she said dryly. "Have a seat."

He sat down beside her on the sofa and ran his fingers through his still-damp hair.

"Sorry." He gave her a rueful look that tugged at her heart. He looked so... alone. So lost. As if he were standing on the edge of a precipice and the ground was crumbling beneath his feet.

Impulsively she touched his forearm, wanting to comfort him. His skin was warm, and she could feel the firm muscles beneath it.

"Cheer up. It could be worse," she offered, mentally wincing at how trite her words sounded.

"That is not a concept I want to explore. What I'm dealing with is bad enough."

Getting to his feet, Kynan wandered over to the patio doors and, twitching aside the beige curtains, peered outside, squinting slightly at the bright morning sunlight.

"Like boxes. All cramped together with no space to breathe," he muttered as a feeling of bleakness settled over him like a shroud. Even the architecture was wrong in this world. And the people...they were so violent, so irrational.

"Different strokes for different folks," Jenna said. "Simply because these houses don't appeal to you is no reason to assume they don't appeal to anyone."

He glanced over his shoulder at her. Jenna Farron wasn't violent. Or irrational. She was logical, intelligent and compassionate. The thought soothed the panic seething beneath the surface of his mind. Dressed differently, she might have come straight out of his world.

"I stand corrected," he finally said. "But I still don't like them."

Jenna shrugged. "Come to that, neither do I. But this house is functional, and it fills my needs. What kind of dwellings did you have?"

"Functional and aesthetically pleasing.

"I wonder where they are," he said, staring up at the sky.

"Where who are?"

"The Atlanteans who left in the spaceships. They're out there somewhere." His face hardened into purposeful lines. "I've got to make contact with them, or I'll be stuck in this hell the rest of my life."

Jenna's gaze dropped from his taut features to his hands, which were curled into fists. She needed to distract him from his unhappy thoughts. Food would do for the moment.

"You need some breakfast," she said. "What did you normally eat?"

"Cereals, fruits," he answered absently.

"Cereal it is." Jenna hurried out to her tiny kitchen. It only took her a few minutes to pour him a bowl of bran flakes, cut a banana into it and add milk.

She carefully brought the slightly full bowl back into the living room and set it down on the coffee table. Kynan was still standing in front of the patio doors, staring outside.

"Come and eat before it gets soggy," she ordered.

Kynan walked over and looked at her offering. Cautiously, he picked up the spoon and took a taste. "Not bad," he pronounced, taking a second bite.

When Kynan had finished, he carried his empty bowl to the kitchen. Jenna watched from the doorway as he placed it on the counter. A man who didn't expect to be waited on, she thought approvingly. Maybe Kynan was right about this vanished civilization of his being a paradise lost.

"I need to get started," he said.

"On what?"

"On sorting through those boxes I brought from the chamber. I want to see how usable the equipment is."

"Um, I hate to rain on your parade," Jenna said as she followed him out to the garage.

"Rain on..." His eyes narrowed as if he were sifting through a dictionary and then his expression lightened. "Ah, I see. You hate to discourage me. Rest assured, you do not have the ability to do so."

Was that supposed to make her feel better? she wondered ruefully. If so, she had news for him. No woman liked to be told by the most intriguing male she'd ever met that she had no influence over him. Although it was undoubtedly for the best, she assured herself. Getting emotionally involved with Kynan would be a one-way ticket to disaster. That much was crystal clear, even to someone as inexperienced with men as she was.

She looked up to find Kynan watching her.

"I said the wrong thing?" he asked.

"Not if it was what you meant to say."

"But there is a problem." He reached out and grasped her chin between his thumb and forefinger, slowly tilting her chin up. His eyes were swirling with an emotion she couldn't identify, but found infinitely exciting.

"Hypolearning gave me an excellent grasp of your language, but I am still a long way from understanding nuances. And then there is your culture." He lightly stroked his forefinger over her cheek. Tiny rivulets of sensation spread from his gentle caress, tightening her skin.

Jenna blinked, trying to focus on what he was saying and not on what she was feeling. "Culture?" She latched on to the word.

"Hmm." His finger stopped its insidious movement, and he cupped her cheek in his callused palm. "I'm not sure at what a woman in your culture might take offense."

"Oh?" Jenna's voice came out on a breathless sigh.

"Yes. For example..." He leaned closer and his broad shoulders filled her vision, but his size didn't make her feel threatened. On the contrary, it made her feel safe. Secure in a way that was new to her.

"In my culture a man could do this." Kynan gently brushed his lips against hers, and a tremor shot through her. The warm, soapy smell of his skin drifted into her lungs, and her eyelids felt heavy. So very heavy. She wanted to close them and lean against him.

"But I do not know if you would find that offensive," he continued.

Jenna could think of a hundred words to describe his kiss, starting with pleasurable and ending with habit-forming. But there wasn't a negative among them.

"No, I don't find it offensive. I fact, I find it a rather pleasant greeting." She tried to sound a lot more sophisticated than she felt.

A quick grin lifted his lips, giving her a glimpse of his straight, white teeth. "Just 'rather'? How would you go about it?"

Jenna stared up into his amused eyes and felt a sense of adventure stir in her. She wanted to kiss him again. She made no attempt to deny the desire swirling through her. And what would be the harm? He certainly didn't look as if he'd object. Did that mean he found her attractive? As attractive as she found him? The thought lent her courage.

"We've developed a few embellishments over the years." Jenna ran her fingertips along his jawline. His skin was smooth and taut. "For example..." Standing on tiptoe, she wrapped her arms around his neck and pressed herself against him, savoring the feel of his hard frame pushing against her much softer one.

"A nice variation," he assured her solemnly. "Do you have any more?"

Not nearly as many as I'd like, Jenna thought ruefully.

Tightening her grip slightly, she tugged his head down and lightly pressed her lips against his. A shivery sensation danced through her. The compulsion to intensify both the kiss and the feeling was almost irresistible, and that worried her. Worried her enough that she retreated, stepping back and putting some distance between them.

"Well," she said brightly, "how about if we cart all this...stuff into the house?"

"All right," he agreed. Jenna wasn't sure if she were disappointed or not by his easy acceptance of her withdrawal.

"Kynan," she said as she watched him effortlessly move a stack of boxes with the aid of his antigravity device, "did everyone in Atlantis have one of those things?"

"No, there were actually only a handful of them in existence." He maneuvered the boxes through the door into the house. "We were developing them in my lab when the meteorites were discovered and all research was put on hold while we tried to find a way to cope with the catastrophe."

"Can you make more of them?" Jenna asked eagerly. "One of those things would be a godsend to an archaeologist out in the field trying to transport equipment over rough terrain."

"With the right tools and resources I could, but in this culture . . ." His face tightened.

"I'll take some of the smaller boxes." Jenna determinedly changed the subject. She wanted him to concentrate on what he could do, not on what he couldn't.

Twenty minutes later, Kynan had carefully stacked all of his boxes in the living room, using up most of the available floor space. It was a good thing she wasn't claustrophobic, Jenna thought as she looked around her small, cramped living room in resignation.

What Kynan needed was a proper lab for his research, but his chances of getting one anytime soon were not good. She could provide him with a hideout, but she didn't have the resources to equip a lab for him.

Jenna watched him opening boxes with an eagerness that put her in mind of a small boy at Christmas. It was obvious that he felt about his machines as she did about her artifacts. They were a necessary component of his life. She nibbled uncertainly on her lower lip. If she couldn't give him a lab, who could? The government?

A premonition of impending disaster tightened the muscles in her shoulders. Kynan did not seem to be the kind of man who would have much patience with all the rules and regulations governmental bureaucratic types favored. And he certainly didn't have much sympathy for the world those types had created. Maybe she could convince him to be a little more conciliatory? Her gaze lingered on the strong line of his jaw. Then again, maybe she couldn't.

"Ah, there it is!" Kynan's excited voice interrupted her troublesome thoughts, and Jenna was only too glad to let them float away.

"There's what?" Jenna squinted at the machine he was pulling out of a box.

"It allows me to read these." He gestured toward a pile of pale lavender strips on the floor at his feet. "Watch." He inserted one of the strips into the top of the machine, activated something on its side and a crystal-clear image instantly appeared on the living-room wall.

Jenna whistled. "Now that's impressive."

"Yes, that matrix—"

"No, not the picture. The batteries that must power that machine. The bunny's competition would be in seventh heaven to get their hands on anything that lasts that long."

Kynan shrugged. "It's just a rather elementary use of nuclear power."

Jenna blinked. "In my living room!"

Kynan looked at her in surprise. "Why not?"

"My society hasn't been very effective in its use of atomic power."

"Your society has not been very effective in anything!"

"It's your society now, too," she reminded him.

"I'm only passing through." Kynan's words had the ring of a vow.

"Yeah, I know. Like, 'Stop the world, I want to get off.'"

"I will escape. Just as soon as I manage to make contact with the Atlanteans who left."

Jenna was about to point out that if they had survived, they would have returned by now and someone would have noticed them. But she thought better of it. Right now, Kynan didn't need logic. He needed hope. Hope that he could escape from what he felt was an imperfect world. In a few weeks when he was feeling a little more comfortable in this environment, then she'd point out the impossibility of what he was hoping for.

"What exactly—" She began only to break off as the front doorbell rang.

Kynan glanced around the living room, seeking the source of the sound. "What was that?" he asked.

"Someone's at the front door," Jenna said, wondering who it could be. She could count on one hand the visitors she'd had since she'd arrived in El Paso last month. That she should suddenly get one right after Kynan appeared, worried her.

"We used to see who had come to call," Kynan suggested.

"Kynan," she said slowly, "I don't know who that is, but some people might—"

"Consider me a threat?" He grimaced. "Don't worry. I'll be careful."

"You'd do better to be silent. It's safer," she said as the bell sounded again. Reluctantly she went to answer it, closely followed by Kynan. Cautiously she peered through the peephole in the door and then breathed a sigh of relief.

Kynan looked when she stepped back. "Old. Very old," he pronounced.

"Don't you dare say anything about her age," Jenna hissed. "Mrs. Coltrain is a dear, and I won't have her feelings hurt."

"I wouldn't dream of harming an elder in any way," Kynan assured her.

"Oh, and by the way, you're a visiting professor from Sweden," she told him as she unlatched the security chain.

Kynan looked confused. "Sweden?"

"I had to tell her something. She probably just came by to get a look at you. She's very curious." Jenna swung the door open.

"Good morning, Mrs. Coltrain," Jenna said. She was about to add an invitation to come in when she realized that she couldn't. Kynan's boxes were all over the living room. Mrs. Coltrain might be old, but she wasn't the least bit senile. She'd know at once that there was something very strange about those boxes.

"Oh, Jenna, I'm sorry to bother you, but I don't know what to do. I called the fire department, but they said that they only did that in movies, not in real life."

Jenna blinked, completely lost. The only thing she understood was that Mrs. Coltrain was extremely agitated, and it couldn't be good for her, not at her age.

"Take a deep breath, Mrs. Coltrain," Jenna ordered, "and then tell my why you need the fire department."

"For Eleanor Roosevelt," Mrs. Coltrain's voice wavered.

"Eleanor Roosevelt?" Jenna asked, not understanding.

"Wife of the thirty-second president of the United States. Deceased," Kynan rattled off helpfully.

Mrs. Coltrain nodded. "Unfortunately, yes. But in my opinion she was the greatest woman of the twentieth century. That's why I named my own dear Eleanor after her."

"Eleanor is Mrs. Coltrain's cat," Jenna told Kynan. "Mrs. Coltrain, this is my colleague, Kynan—" Jenna mentally scrambled for a Swedish-sounding surname "—Anderson."

"How do you do?" Mrs. Coltrain nodded distractedly at him.

"Why is your cat of concern to you?" Kynan cut to the heart of the matter.

"She climbed a tree and can't get down." Mrs. Coltrain wrung her hands in dismay. "I'm so afraid she'll fall."

"Highly unlikely," Kynan said. "If she got up, she can get down."

"Eleanor is very sensitive," Mrs. Coltrain insisted. "I got her from the pound, you know."

"Don't worry," Jenna hurriedly inserted before Kynan could blurt out anything that might reveal his unfamiliarity with rather normal institutions. "I'll help."

"Oh, thank you. I didn't want to bother you when you had company, but I just didn't know what to do. She's in that big tree in my backyard." Mrs. Coltrain turned and started toward her home.

"Wait here, I'll be right back," Jenna told Kynan.

"No. You might need me. Besides, I want to see this cat. The species must have evolved a lot since Atlantis if they're now so sensitive."

"I doubt they've changed one bit. And you can't come." Jenna glanced at Mrs. Coltrain who had stopped at the curb and was waiting for her. "Something might happen."

"Not to me. I used to climb mountains." He hurried after Mrs. Coltrain.

Giving up, Jenna trotted after him. Short of grabbing him by his shirttail and trying to stuff him back into the house, there was nothing she could do. Jenna studied the breadth of his shoulders. She had about as much chance of physically forcing her will on him as he had of contacting those missing Atlanteans.

Mrs. Coltrain did tend to be a little absentminded at times. Maybe she wouldn't notice if Kynan made a mistake, Jenna thought hopefully. Or, perhaps, she'd simply put it down to his being a foreigner.

"It was the man from the gas company, you know," Mrs. Coltrain confided as she unlatched the side gate into her backyard. "He came into the yard to read the meter and frightened Eleanor. There's the poor dear." Mrs. Coltrain pointed to the top of the tree.

Kynan eyed the tree consideringly. "It's not very tall."

"It is if you're only a foot high," Mrs. Coltrain said reproachfully.

"No problem." Jenna grabbed hold of the lowest branch and hoisted herself up into the tree. "You wait here," she told Kynan. He might look a hundred percent better than when she'd first found him, but looks could be deceptive.

She didn't want to risk him having a dizzy spell and slipping.

"But—"

"You can catch me if I fall," Jenna said and then cautiously began to work her way toward the outraged ball of orange fluff about ten feet above her.

"Nice kitty," Jenna crooned soothingly.

Eleanor wasn't impressed. She arched her back and hissed furiously.

"Stupid Eleanor," Jenna muttered under her breath as she slowly inched out on the limb after the cat.

"Go to Jenna, dear. Jenna likes Eleanor," Mrs. Coltrain shouted encouragingly from the ground.

Jenna slowly reached toward the cat, trying not to startle it. She wasn't successful. Eleanor gave a howl of anger and swiped at her with a lethal-looking set of claws. Jenna instinctively jerked back and slipped off her precarious perch.

"Jenna!" Mrs. Coltrain wailed from below while Jenna frantically grabbed for something to break her fall. Rescue came as her silk blouse was suddenly snagged on a broken limb. There was a sound of tearing material and then she was caught securely.

Jenna's first reaction was relief that she wasn't going to wind up a crumpled mass of broken bones on the rock-hard ground below. Her second was annoyance when Eleanor moved to within two feet of her, sat on her haunches and eyed her disdainfully.

"Just you wait. You'll get yours," Jenna muttered. She started to reach for the cat, only to discover that she was firmly caught by the branch. She twisted, trying to reach behind herself to pull her blouse free, but she couldn't quite manage it.

Jenna stifled the urge to scream in frustration. As far as she could see, she had two choices: continue to hang there like an oversize Christmas-tree ornament or unbutton her blouse and climb down. In her semitransparent bra. Jenna looked down to find Kynan watching her. She could see the corners of his mouth twitching in amusement. What would Kynan think of her fancy silk bra? The thought unexpectedly popped into her mind. Would he find it exciting? A feeling of heat surged beneath her skin.

"Are you all right, Jenna?" Mrs. Coltrain called up.

"Fine," Jenna assured her. "I just seem to be a little stuck."

"You should have let me do it in the first place," Kynan said. Grabbing hold of a branch, he swung himself up with a lithe grace.

Jenna glared at him through the leafy green branches. "You say one word about male superiority..."

He looked vaguely confused by her words. "I was referring to the fact that I told you I climb mountains."

"Probably because he's Swedish," Mrs. Coltrain offered peaceably. "Or is it one of the other Scandinavian countries that have all those mountains? No matter. At least he'll be able to get you free."

Kynan climbed onto the limb beneath her and, bracing himself, reached for her. He managed to grasp the tail of her bright pink shirt in his fingertips and with one jerk ripped it free.

"You climb down, and I'll get Eleanor," Kynan told her.

Jenna looked into his amused eyes and a smoldering warmth oozed through her. He looked so alive. So quintessentially masculine. And he was looking at her as if he found her a very desirable woman. She wasn't used to men finding her physically attractive. The vast majority of men she'd known had been too intimidated by her intellect to see her as a woman.

Jenna stifled a sigh as she carefully climbed down. Just her luck. She finally found a man who wasn't the least bit daunted by her intelligence—and all he wanted to do was to get off the world.

Once she was safely back on the ground, Jenna watched as Kynan reached for the cat. Eleanor stared at his approaching hand with an unblinking gaze and then sprang with a shriek that would have given Jack the Ripper pause. Kynan jerked back as the cat landed on his chest, viciously digging her claws into his flesh as she scrambled over him and raced down the tree.

Jenna winced. She'd been the victim of Eleanor's claws herself, and she knew how painful they were.

"Oh, my poor baby," Mrs. Coltrain crooned as Eleanor jumped out of the tree and streaked for the old woman. The cat leaped into Mrs. Coltrain's arms and turned to give Jenna a smirk.

"Thank you both so much," Mrs. Coltrain said as Kynan swung down to the ground. "I don't know what I would have done without you."

"No problem," Jenna lied with a worried glance at the droplets of blood staining the front of Kynan's shirt.

"Come into the house, Eleanor, and I'll give you a nice plate of tuna to help you get over your fright," Mrs. Coltrain told the cat. "Would you and Kynan like a cup of coffee, Jenna?"

"No, thank you," Jenna refused. She wanted to get Kynan home and put antiseptic on his wounds.

"Later, then." Mrs. Coltrain said absently, her attention clearly focused on her cat. "Please make sure the gate is closed as you leave." She turned and hurried into her house.

Kynan watched the door close behind her and then said, "Fascinating."

"Not quite the adjective I would have used." Jenna headed toward the open gate. "I wonder how susceptible you are to modern germs?" she worried out loud.

"If I can survive the people, the germs can't be much of a problem. Does Mrs. Coltrain really harbor affection for that monster?"

"Mrs. Coltrain worships the ground that antisocial fiend treads on," Jenna assured him. "And don't ask me why. Except for her inexplicable love for Eleanor, she's perfectly rational. I—" Jenna broke off as she saw the white car with an official emblem of some sort on the side, parked in front of her house.

"What's wrong?" Kynan noticed her unease.

Jenna felt her stomach clutch in sudden fear as a man climbed out of the car and walked toward her front door. He was wearing a dark green uniform. What did the Army want with her? Common sense said that it had something to do with Kynan.

Unconsciously she squared her shoulders. There was no way she was going to tamely hand Kynan over without a fight.

"Don't say anything," she muttered to Kynan. "Let me do the talking."

"He's dressed in a uniform?" Kynan picked up on the relevant point.

"Army. But he can't know anything," she said, praying it was true.

"May I help you?" Jenna took the initiative when they reached the man.

"I'm looking for a Dr. Farron."

"I'm Dr. Farron. And you are?"

"Colonel Macintosh." He held out his hand, and Jenna hastily shook it, hoping that Kynan would pick up on the custom. To her relief, he did.

"This is Dr. Anderson, a visiting professor from Sweden." Jenna gave the colonel the same cover story she'd given Mrs. Coltrain.

"Sweden?" Macintosh gave Kynan a cursory look.

"Yes, he's perfecting his English before the start of the fall term," Jenna decided to provide excuses in advance. "What was it you wanted to see me about?"

"I got your name from Bob Lessing out at the Circle Q Ranch."

"Oh?" Jenna said noncommittally. Had they found the hidden chamber despite Kynan's attempts to camouflage the entrance?

"Yes, Lessing says you've been spending a great deal of time this past month on his ranch, Dr. Farron."

"I've been searching for artifacts that I hope will give us some clues as to the specific nature of the Indians who lived in this area before the Spanish arrived," Jenna told him truthfully. "But why would my archaeological activities be of interest to the Army? Have I inadvertently wandered onto one of your bases?" She tried to look suitably shocked.

"Trespassing isn't my concern. I'm trying to pin down the reason for some interference in our radar Tuesday night."

The night she'd found Kynan. And also the night he'd been operating the huge machine, she remembered with a sinking feeling.

Deciding that a good offense might well be the best defense, she said, "Do you think I interfered with your transmissions?"

"No, ma'am," Macintosh said. "I simply want to know if you have seen anything unusual in your exploration of the desert."

Jenna counted to ten to make it appear that she was considering the question and then said, "No. It's pretty deserted out there. Just snakes and scorpions.

"What do you think might have caused your problem?" Jenna felt the question might seem normal.

"Probably just a natural phenomenon," Macintosh answered, falling back on the old standby.

Kynan was a phenomenon, all right, Jenna thought ruefully. How natural he was, remained to be seen.

"What about you, Dr. Anderson?" Macintosh turned to Kynan.

"What?" Kynan gave him a vacant smile.

"Did you see anything out in the desert?" Macintosh asked impatiently.

"He hasn't been out in the desert," Jenna hurriedly inserted. "He isn't interested in archaeology. He's visiting me."

"Oh?" Macintosh studied Kynan. "What is your field, Dr. Anderson?"

"Engineering," Jenna quickly replied. "If I can be of any more help to you, Colonel, feel free to call."

"Of course." Macintosh took the hint and walked back to his car. He slipped behind the wheel and, starting the car, automatically flipped on the air-conditioning. He felt as if he couldn't breathe in the stifling heat. He rubbed his hand over his chest, trying to ease the pain burning there. It didn't help. Nothing did. He gripped the steering wheel in frustration and fear.

It was becoming increasingly clear that the angioplasty hadn't worked. He could feel the crushing pain in his chest getting worse, day by day. But if he told the doctor, he'd undoubtedly want to do bypass surgery. And the Army would probably use that as an excuse to force him into early retirement.

Even if he didn't voluntarily say anything to the doctor, he wasn't going to be able to hide his condition much longer. As soon as he reported for his checkup week after next, the surgeon would find out just how badly the procedure had failed.

What was he going to do? The Army was his whole life. Without it he didn't have anything. A feeling of panic tightened the vise around his chest.

Calm, think calm. He forced himself to focus on an empty soda can sitting in the gutter. He still had over two weeks left. And he had this assignment to handle. He glanced back at the door Dr. Farron and her inarticulate Swede had disappeared through. He had a bad feeling about that pair, even though he couldn't quite put his finger on what it was exactly that was bothering him.

All he knew for certain was that alarms had gone off in his mind when he'd discovered that Lessing had given some archaeologist permission to roam his land. A fact that made no sense, given what he'd been told about Lessing's suspected drug activities.

What's more, neither of them had been the slightest help, just like absolutely everyone else he'd talked to in this case.

He had expected Lessing to be evasive, given his ties to the drug cartel, but none of the other ranchers living in the area had been willing to tell him anything. Because there was nothing to tell? Or because they were afraid.

Could they know what Lessing was up to and automatically assume that anything unusual was connected with drug smuggling? That would certainly explain their silence. No rational man tangled with a drug cartel. But a desperate one might. An idea suddenly occurred to him, as he pulled into the road.

If he could nail a gang of drug smugglers, it would give him so much publicity the Army wouldn't dare try to force him into early retirement. It just might be possible. He carefully weighed the situation. Investigating the flying-saucer report gave him an ideal cover behind which to operate. One determined man with nothing to lose and everything to gain might be able to pull it off. He felt his first glimmer of real hope since his condition had been diagnosed.

He stopped at the corner and glanced in his rearview mirror at Dr. Farron's house. Maybe he could get her to give him a guided tour over the area where she'd been working. Asking for her help wouldn't seem an unreasonable thing to do and it would give him a chance to take a good look around Lessing's ranch without being obvious about what he was looking for.

He did a U-turn at the intersection, parked a few houses from Dr. Farron's and cut the engine. He'd just wait a few minutes until the worst of the pain in his chest subsided. Then he'd go back and ask Dr. Farron when she was going out into the desert again.

Four

"**W**hat is his function?" Kynan peered over Jenna's shoulder as she furtively watched Macintosh sitting in his car through the crack in the bedroom curtains.

"Function?" Jenna's shoulders slumped in relief as Macintosh finally pulled away from the curb.

"What does he do?"

"At a guess, I'd say he chases rumors. But the fact that he's a bird colonel bothers me," she said slowly.

Kynan stared blankly at her. "What kind of bird?"

Jenna moved away from the window. "It's a rank, and the bird refers to the eagle on his uniform. I wouldn't think that someone that high up would normally be chasing rumors about strange lights in the desert. Or even radar malfunctions, for that matter. They must be very worried if they sent a full colonel."

"Unfortunate." Kynan shrugged, wincing at the movement.

"That blasted cat." Jenna reacted to Kynan's obvious discomfort. "Heaven only knows where she's been. Sit down on the bed while I go get something from the medicine cabinet to put on your scratches."

She grabbed a lemon-yellow T-shirt out of the bureau to replace the shirt she'd ripped and headed for the bathroom.

"Mrs. Coltrain reminds me of someone from my time," Kynan said when Jenna returned a few minutes later. "A very old woman named Ephia who was inexplicably devoted to a kind of poisonous lizard."

Jenna uncapped the tube of ointment. "I don't imagine people have changed all that much."

"Ha!"

"Not basically," she insisted. "Surely your culture had its antisocial elements, too?"

"We had a different definition of antisocial," Kynan said dryly. "We had not had what you call a murder in over two thousand years."

Jenna eyed him thoughtfully, wondering whether or not to believe him. It didn't seem possible that mankind could once have been so civilized, and yet, if it was true, that would explain Kynan's total revulsion to what he'd seen on the news. It was also possible that he was remembering what he wanted to be true. Or that his memory had been damaged by the process that had kept him in a state of suspended animation all these years.

On the other hand, his memory was quite accurate about some things. She remembered his competent manipulation of the huge machine in the cave as well as his use of the antigravity device when they'd moved the boxes. But at the moment, she was more concerned about his physical wellbeing than his memory.

"If you'd take off your shirt so that I can see what the damage is?" she asked, watching as he began to slip the buttons free. Each one he released gave her a better view of his chest and the thick mat of reddish-golden hair that covered it.

Jenna remembered listening to an interview with a famous stripper who'd claimed that her being naked wasn't the real turn-on for her audience, but rather, *how* she got naked. At the time, Jenna had thought it was a naive statement, but now she wasn't so sure. Just watching Kynan do nothing more than unbutton his shirt was sending her blood pressure skyrocketing.

She waited, filled with a sense of breathless anticipation as he shrugged out of the shirt. Engrossed, Jenna watched his muscles ripple at the movement, and her eyes wandered slowly over the breadth of his shoulders. Her absorption was abruptly shattered when she noticed the raw, angry scratch that ran from the base of his neck across his right collarbone.

"Nasty," she said.

"It's just a scratch."

Jenna chuckled. "You sound like the lead in a bad spaghetti Western."

"And you sound incomprehensible. Just put your antiseptic on and be done with it."

Jenna obligingly squeezed some of the salve onto her fingertip and gently began to rub it into the scratch. She finished rubbing in the ointment and then indulged her compulsive desire to touch him by lightly trailing her hand over his chest as if looking for other wounds.

"Is this part of the cure?" Kynan's voice sounded huskier than usual.

Maybe touching him would be a cure, she thought dreamily. A cure for her inexplicable fascination with his body. Maybe if she were to indulge it, it would lose its intensity. Or deepen, the appalling thought occurred to her; but she refused to spoil the present by worrying about the future.

"I'm looking for other scratches," she said, being careful to avoid touching the crystal device hanging over his heart. The fact that she could never quite get a clear view of it made her very leery.

"Actually, I think my scratch needs more than just an ointment."

Was Kynan more susceptible to disease than a modern person? Jenna wondered, as fear drove all thoughts of the crystal out of her mind. "What does it need?" she asked apprehensively.

"Psychological reinforcement."

Jenna relaxed, her apprehension dissolving beneath the gleam of humor she could see glittering in Kynan's eyes. "What kind of psychological reinforcement?"

"It is a known fact that the human body heals far more quickly when the mind is relaxed."

Jenna grinned at him. "*I* don't know that."

"Of course you do. I just told you so."

"No, you gave me a theory. It has yet to be proven."

Kynan's lips lifted in a tantalizing smile. "I'm always in favor of scientific research."

Feeling greatly daring, Jenna trailed a fingertip along his jawline. "And what would it take to relax your mind?"

Kynan stared at the wall as if thinking about it. Suddenly, with no warning, he grabbed her and pulled her down onto his lap.

Jenna gave a squeak of surprise as she landed across his hard thighs. They seemed to burn her soft hips, and she wiggled slightly to intensify the sensation. His response was immediate and unmistakable. Did that mean he was as fascinated with her as she was with him? It was an intoxicating thought that bubbled through her veins like a potent champagne.

"What are you doing?" she asked.

"I told you. I'm relaxing my body." His arms closed around her, and he pulled her closer to his bare chest.

Jenna gulped. He might consider this relaxing, but as far as she was concerned, what he was doing to her caused extreme agitation.

He gently pushed her head back against his shoulder, and Jenna peered up through her thick lashes, focusing on his firm lips. She wanted to taste them. She wanted to explore.... Her thoughts scattered as he swooped down and captured her mouth. A rush of feeling swirled through her, heightening her senses and making her aware of him in every pore of her body. Jenna snuggled deeper into his embrace, blindly seeking to intensify what she was feeling. To her acute disappointment, Kynan lifted his head and, placing a last, quick kiss on her throbbing lips, lifted her to her feet.

Jenna grabbed the edge of the headboard as she frantically struggled to rein in her chaotic emotions. She didn't want Kynan to realize just how violently she had responded to what had really been a relatively chaste kiss. She wanted him to think that she was as sophisticated as he appeared to be. If he were to realize just how inexperienced she was, he might well decide to back off. And she couldn't bear the thought of not getting to kiss him again. And again.

Think of him as just another colleague, she tried to tell herself. It didn't help. He didn't remind her even vaguely of anyone she worked with—but she'd sure like to, she thought wistfully. Maybe she could help get him an appointment teaching ancient history at the university. He certainly had the background for it.

"Now then, where were we?" he said as he shrugged on his shirt.

Jenna watched with a sense of loss as he rebuttoned it.

"Ah, yes, you were going to take me back to the cave." His unexpected announcement effectively shook her free of her erotic thoughts.

"That's news to me. Why do you want to go back there? Especially now that the military's sniffing around?"

"I have to," Kynan insisted. "I didn't bring everything I need to build the transmitter to contact the other Atlanteans."

Frustrated, Jenna stared into his determined face. This was crazy. Kynan wanted to risk returning to the scene of the crime—so to speak—to get parts to build a transmitter to contact people who didn't exist.

Kynan stared back at Jenna, his sense of frustration matching her own. Somehow he had to make her understand how important building the transmitter was. He couldn't stay in this world. It wasn't her.... His expression unconsciously softened as he remembered the trusting way she'd nestled against him. No, she wasn't the problem. If this world had been filled with people as intelligent and warm and caring as she, he'd have resigned himself to making a life here. But from what he'd seen on the newscasts, people like Jenna Farron were few and far between.

He clenched his teeth together as he fought to stem the panic that threatened to overwhelm him. He had to escape, and the only way to do that was to contact the descendants of the Atlanteans who'd left in the spaceships.

"Jenna, I have to do this. If you won't help me...." His voice trailed away, but Jenna had no trouble reading the determined jut of his chin.

If she wouldn't help him, he'd try himself, she mentally finished his sentence. And despite the fact that his fancy machine had given him an unbelievable command of her language, as well as a jumbled assortment of historical facts, it couldn't have given him the knowledge of her culture he needed to survive. There was so much he didn't know. Simple things like the fact that it wasn't safe to roam certain areas of any big city after dark. He could easily wind up shot because he wouldn't realize the danger until it was too late.

The thought of his lifeless body sprawled on a sidewalk somewhere made her feel faintly desperate. She couldn't risk that happening. Not matter how illogical Kynan's desire to go back into the desert was, she had to help him.

"All right." She threw up her hands in defeat. "I'll take you."

"Now?" Kynan peered hopefully at her.

Jenna stifled the impulse to stall and tried to consider the situation logically. "Yes, I think so," she finally said. "I've been spending my days in the desert since I got here. So going now would simply be following my normal pattern and shouldn't make anyone suspicious." I hope, she added under her breath.

"Fine. Let's go." Kynan headed toward the garage.

"You would have loved Shakespeare," Jenna muttered as she followed him.

"Why would I have been enamored of an English dramatist who has been dead for four hundred years?"

"He was the one who said, 'If it were done...'twere well it were done quickly.'" She checked the bed of the truck to make sure that her supplies hadn't been inadvertently unpacked earlier. They were still there.

Reluctantly she climbed into the cab, unable to shake the feeling that this was a bad idea. A very bad idea. But one that she was committed to carrying through, she reminded herself.

"Isn't that the colonel we talked to?" Kynan asked as Jenna pulled into the street.

"What!" Jenna looked in the direction Kynan was pointing, praying he was wrong. He wasn't. She had a clear view of both the colonel's car with its military plates as well as the colonel himself. Why had he come back? Because he hadn't been satisfied with the answers she'd given him? The appalling thought occurred to her.

Jenna watched nervously as Macintosh started his car and slipped into the traffic behind them. "I wonder if I can lose him."

Kynan checked in the side view mirror. "How? He doesn't look very losable."

"It works in the movies." Jenna turned south onto Montana Street. "We'll go downtown and try to shake him in the heavy traffic and the jaywalkers. Then we'll cut back on the side roads, pick up the expressway and head out to the cave."

To Jenna's relief her plan worked to perfection. As usual, the downtown area was a mass of people weaving in and out of the bumper-to-bumper traffic. She deliberately slowed down as she approached a yellow traffic light. The second it turned red, she sent up a silent prayer that there was no cop in the area, stepped on the gas and ran it, leaving Macintosh trapped two cars behind her. Five minutes later, she was on the Patriot Freeway, heading into the desert.

"It seems to have worked. He isn't anywhere around us." Kynan turned from his study of the sparse traffic behind them.

"I just hope he doesn't realize we were aware he was following us. That way he won't think I deliberately gave him the slip. Maybe he'll just think I'm a reckless driver."

Kynan grabbed hold of his shoulder strap as she quickly turned off the highway. "Now why would he think that?" he asked dryly. "Maybe you ought to show me how to operate this vehicle."

And then Kynan would come and go as he pleased. And who knew what trouble he inadvertently might get into. "Why bother?" she finally said. "You're going to be leaving just as soon as you make contact with your fellow Atlanteans."

"Yes, but this mode of transportation fascinates me. It seems to be so highly inefficient."

Jenna shrugged. "You can't prove it by me. I don't know much about machines."

"What precisely do you know about?" Kynan asked curiously.

"The past. I try to reconstruct the past using artifacts, legends, myths and the like."

"We had individuals who were interested in that field of study," he said thoughtfully. "But they were at Quxocty for the most part."

Jenna looked at him in sudden interest and then hastily returned her attention to the road when the truck lurched to the left as it hit a huge chuckhole. "Your past would really be past. I'll bet it was fascinating," she said enviously.

"The past is totally unproductive. What difference does it make if we really came from the stars like our legends claimed?"

"What!" Jenna stared at him in shock.

"Our legends say that we were survivors fleeing an inter-stellar holocaust, and we took refuge on Earth. But that was all a long time ago and there was no hard evidence to support the theory."

Jenna felt a surge of frustration. "I was definitely born in the wrong time," she muttered.

"Not from my perspective. I don't know what would have happened if you hadn't been here to help me."

Jenna felt a warm glow envelop her at his words. She just hoped nothing interfered with her continued help, such as Colonel Macintosh.

Pushing all thoughts of the future to the back of her mind, she concentrated on driving over what was little more than a cattle trail through the scrub. When she reached the spot where she'd parked the day she'd found him, she stopped and turned off the engine.

"Kynan, did you bring that antigravity device of yours?"

"Yes. Why?"

"Because I don't want to drive the truck any closer to your cave. Someone might follow the tire tracks."

Reaching into the glove compartment, she pulled out the hat she normally wore, as well as her spare. "Here." She handed Kynan an Australian slouch hat. "Wear this."

Kynan took the hat and turned it around in his hands curiously. "Why?" he finally asked.

"Because that sun is strong enough to blister paint, and I don't need you to come down with sunstroke."

"Unnecessary. I'm not bothered by the sun."

"Humor me." She jammed her own on her head. To her relief, Kynan followed suit. He looked fantastic in that hat, she thought, intrigued by the way the brim partially hid his eyes. He could make a fortune as a male model.

Kynan pulled a small instrument out of his pocket and studied the pattern of symbols moving across it.

"What's that?" Jenna asked.

"A homing device," he said absently as he climbed out of the cab. Turning to his left, he took off at a trot. Jenna hurried after him, hoping that they wouldn't find a reception committee.

They didn't. There was no one at the cave, nor could Jenna see any sign that anyone had been there in their absence.

Fortunately for Jenna's peace of mind, Kynan showed no disposition to linger. He quickly assembled what he wanted to take and stacked the items by the door. Three trips from the cave to the truck and four hours later, they were back in Jenna's garage.

It took them another thirty minutes to move the boxes into her living room where Kynan stacked them on top of the ones already there. Jenna straightened, rubbing her tired back. She felt hot, sweaty and gritty. She wanted a shower and something to eat, in that order.

She looked over to where Kynan was sorting through the boxes, his expression totally absorbed. What would it be like to have him look at her with that engrossed fascination? she wondered. To have him respond to her as if she were the beginning and the end of his world?

What was the matter with her? she wondered uneasily. She'd never before spent her time daydreaming about a man. At least, not about a man that hadn't been dead for at least a few thousand years—she remembered her teenage infatuation with Alexander the Great. So, what was it about Kynan that drew her?

She watched as the sunlight pouring in through the patio doors engulfed him in a golden haze. He looked exactly like a Michelangelo painting of an archangel. But there was nothing ethereal about Kynan. Her gaze lingered on the muscles of his arms, which bulged as he rearranged his boxes.

"Kynan? Kynan!" she repeated.

He looked up and blinked as if surprised to find himself where he was.

"Yes?"

"I'm going to take a shower, and then I'll fix us something to eat. If anyone knocks on the door, don't answer it."

"But what if it's Mrs. Coltrain? She might need something."

"True," Jenna conceded. "Tell you what, look through the peephole. If it is Mrs. Coltrain, answer it. But be careful what you say."

Kynan nodded and went back to his sorting while Jenna hurried into the bathroom. She closed the door behind her and automatically stripped out of her dusty clothes, her mind taken up with the incredible idea that man might not have originated on Earth. As she hurried through her shower, eager to get back to him, she wondered what other legends Kynan's people had.

Shoving her fingers through her wet hair, Jenna carelessly pushed the short strands into place and then paused as she caught sight of herself in the large mirror over the bathroom sink. She frowned at her small breasts and boyishly slender hips, wishing for at least the millionth time for a figure that more closely resembled the masculine ideal of feminine.

But did Kynan share her culture's ideal of physical beauty? she wondered, as she began to dress. To say that Kynan was out of step with modern society was the understatement of the year. What kind of woman turned him on? Had there been one particular woman? A sudden chill feathered over her skin and she shivered. Could he still be emotionally attached to someone?

Probably not, she reassured herself, or he wouldn't have kissed her. And he'd kissed her as if he'd thoroughly enjoyed doing it, too. The thought warmed her. He wouldn't have done that if he'd been in love with someone else. But did he even believe in love? She chewed uncertainly on her lower lip. The concept of romantic love was a relatively new one as far as society went. Maybe his culture hadn't had it?

She tilted her head to one side as she heard a popping sound echoing through the bathroom door. "Uh-oh," she muttered as she hastily finished dressing. What had Kynan unleashed in her living room?

The sound came again. Louder this time and it sounded like . . . an explosion? A gunshot? Colonel Macintosh! Jenna's stomach plummeted, and she raced toward the kitchen.

She skidded through the doorway, coming to a breathless halt when she realized that Kynan was by himself.

He was standing in front of the sink holding a reddish-orange tube about six inches long.

Curious, Jenna came closer and peered around him into the sink. The dirty dishes that had filled it earlier were now gone. Replaced by what looked to be fragments of . . . blue pottery.

Jenna turned and looked from Kynan to the tube he was holding and then back to the sink. "Tell me, was that pile of rubble once my dishes?"

Kynan set the tube down on the counter and stared at the mess. "They're rather fragile, aren't they?" he finally said.

"Not anymore they aren't," she said wryly. "Now they look like something I'd dig up in my line of work. Just tell me why."

He shoved his fingers through his rumpled hair. "I wanted to help. You said that you were going to fix us something to eat, and we still hadn't done anything about the remains from our last meal."

"Well, you certainly did something. Since I assume that you didn't intend to reduce the dishes to rubble, what was the purpose of that—" she waved at the tube "—thing?"

"It controls vibrations. I thought it would simply vibrate the clinging bits of food off the dishes."

Jenna gave him a rueful grin, sympathizing with his chagrined expression. She remembered often during her childhood she had tried to help, only to make the situation worse, as her annoyed parents had been so quick to point out.

"Thanks for the thought anyway," she said. "After dinner, I'll show you a safer way to get them clean."

"Soon?" He gave her a hopeful look.

"Sure. I'll call out for pizza. In the meantime how about a snack?" She opened the freezer and took out a quart of her favorite cappuccino ice cream.

"What's that?" He watched as she scooped some out.

"Ice cream. Try it." She handed him a bowl.

Kynan cautiously tasted it. A rapt expression crossed his face and he took a larger bite. "This is fantastic," he enthused. "We didn't have anything this good in Atlantis."

"Ha! Mark this day on the calendar with a gold star! My culture finally did one thing better than yours."

"Two," Kynan corrected her. "You are more interesting than any woman I ever met in my world. Of course, I didn't meet all that many women," he added meditatively.

Jenna ignored his qualification in favor of savoring the compliment. Kynan thought she was interesting. More interesting than anyone from his own time. The thought made her feel euphoric. She watched tenderly as he wolfed down his ice cream.

Her happy feeling was doused as the sound of the doorbell suddenly echoed through the tiny house. She stepped into the hallway and stared at the front door, trying to decide what to do. If Macintosh had come back here after they'd given him the slip and waited for them to return, he'd know they were here. And if she didn't answer the door, it would make him suspicious.

But if she did answer, then she ran the risk of Kynan inadvertently saying something to make Macintosh even more suspicious.

The doorbell rang again, this time followed by a knock. Whoever it was, was certainly impatient. Like the authorities tended to be.

She turned to Kynan and, motioning for him to be quiet, crept to the door to peer through the peephole. Her tense muscles sagged in relief when she caught sight of the teenage paperboy.

She hastily pulled open the door. "Good afternoon, Bryan. Just a minute while I get my purse."

"Sure, Miss Farron." Bryan leaned against the door frame while Jenna went to find her purse. It took her almost five minutes. It had somehow gotten pushed behind one of Kynan's stacks of boxes. She hastily tugged it free and, opening it, extracted the money for the week's paper as well as a hefty tip for his wait.

When she returned, she found Bryan deep in conversation with Kynan, and a prickle of apprehension slithered over her skin. She wondered uneasily what they were talking about so earnestly. Something that Bryan might repeat to Macintosh if the colonel should start to interview the people she knew?

"Sorry to keep you waiting, Bryan." Jenna handed the teenager his money.

"No problem, Miss Farron. I was just discussing Fizeau's laws with Kynan. Thanks," he added enthusiastically when he saw how much she'd given him. "See you next week." With a careless wave, he cut across her front yard to the next house.

Jenna turned to Kynan. "Fizeau's laws?"

"According to Bryan, Fizeau was the first to recalculate the velocity of light. A most intelligent individual," Kynan added thoughtfully.

Jenna breathed a sigh of relief. Dead physicists were no danger to her. Or anyone else, for that matter. "Never having heard of him, I wouldn't know." She closed the door and carefully bolted it.

"No, not Fizeau. Bryan."

"He seems like a nice young man."

"He has a very ordered mind," Kynan corrected her. "He would be an asset to the scientific community."

"Would?" Jenna asked curiously. "Why not will?"

"Because from what he said, there seems to be little chance that he will acquire the training he needs. Is it true that the individual must pay for his own education?"

"Yes, with a few exceptions."

"But why?" Kynan demanded. "That makes no sense. Society will be the one to benefit from his research. Why should not society pay for his education?"

Jenna shrugged. "Don't glare at me. I happen to agree with you. Unfortunately, that's the way it is."

"The system is wrong," Kynan said flatly. "Even worse, it is grossly inefficient. Someone ought to do something."

"How about you?"

Kynan blinked. "Me?"

"Sure. Bryan's problem is lack of money and—"

"I don't have any money."

"No," Jenna agreed. "But you have the means to acquire money. If you were to patent one of those exotic things of yours—" she gestured toward the boxes littering her living room ''—you could use the proceeds to pay for the education of bright kids like Bryan.''

"An interesting idea. But I won't be here long enough to implement it. Is there any more of this ice cream left?'' he asked, changing the subject.

"In the freezer. Help yourself.''

Jenna called to order their pizza and then decided to watch the evening news while they waited. She spent a few minutes in a futile search among the boxes for the remote control before giving it up as a lost cause and turned the television on by hand. She looked around for a place to sit, but the couch was covered with Kynan's boxes. The room's only chair had just one smallish box on it, so she tugged it onto the floor and sat down.

"The Triple Chocolate Overload ice cream was even better than the first flavor,'' Kynan enthused as he wandered in from the kitchen.

He sat down on the arm of her chair and squinted at the images on the television.

Jenna savored the sensation of his hard thigh pushed against her upper arm. He had the most intriguing body. One she wanted to explore. In great detail.

"What is that?'' Kynan asked.

"A television. It's used mostly for entertainment although it has the potential for education. Did you have something similar?''

"No,'' he said slowly. "What is this about?'' He watched as an image of Hitler haranguing a German crowd filled the screen.

"A clip from the Second World War, which happened about sixty years ago.''

"Recent history,'' Kynan said thoughtfully. He got to his feet and glanced around, looking for a place to sit. He didn't find one so he picked Jenna up out of the chair.

Jenna clutched at his shoulders, her fingers digging into the muscles in his arms to hold herself steady.

He sat down in the chair, settling her onto his lap. "Now we can both watch," he said as he pulled her closer, cradling her slight body against his. The tantalizing scent of some kind of flower clung to her skin, teasing his senses.

He looked down into her night-dark eyes, watching as the pupils enlarged. What would her eyes look like if they were to make love? Would they gleam with pleasure? Would her soft pink lips swell beneath the pressure of his kisses? Or was it too soon to kiss her the way he wanted? Did her culture have some kind of unwritten timetable a man was supposed to follow? he wondered.

Jenna stared up into Kynan's bright eyes as waves of longing rolled over her, interfering with her common sense, which was busily telling her that becoming further involved emotionally with him was trouble with a capital *T*. "What are you thinking?" she asked.

"About how little I know about your customs. Particularly about your sexual mores."

Jenna's heart skipped a beat and then took off at breakneck speed. "Sexual mores?" she repeated, wincing at the breathless quality of her voice. She wanted to appear confident and sophisticated and, instead, she sounded like a naive wallflower faced with the captain of the football team.

"I want to kiss you properly. Leisurely," he said. "How would you view that?"

As the highlight of my nonexistent love life, Jenna thought, but she couldn't quite bring herself to be so honest. "Um, I would view that favorably," she mumbled as her eyes instinctively dropped to his lips. They were a dusky pink color and as she watched, their corners lifted. In humor? Or satisfaction? She couldn't tell, and at the moment she didn't care. All that mattered was that he wanted to kiss her.

His arms tightened around her. Jenna sighed in anticipation and snuggled deeper into his embrace. The heat from his body seeped into her skin, heightening her awareness of him.

He might think this had to do with sexual mores, she thought distractedly. But as far as she was concerned, this was the closest thing to heaven she was ever likely to encounter on Earth and she intended to savor every second of it.

"Hey, Colonel, you found any little green men yet?" one of the men in the post's commissary called after Macintosh as he carefully wove his way through the dinner crowd.

Macintosh mentally winced at the raucous laughter that greeted the question, but he was careful to keep his face blank. Letting Simpson know how much he hated the ribbing would only increase it.

"Not yet," Macintosh said, "but if I do find them and they're looking for a specimen, I'll be sure to point them in your direction."

Macintosh pretended not to notice the gesture from the man seated next to Simpson, inviting him to join them. Instead, he moved across the room toward an empty table near the vending machines.

Reaching it, he sank down into the vinyl chair with a stifled sigh. He took a long swallow of his coffee and tried to ignore the pain eating at his chest. It had reached the point where it was always in the forefront of his mind. He couldn't escape it. Even in sleep, it poisoned his dreams with nightmares.

Damn it! He was only thirty-nine. He wasn't ready for bypass surgery.

"Don't let Simpson get to you," a deep voice ordered as the man slipped into the chair across from Macintosh. "He's an ass."

Macintosh grimaced. "Tell me something I don't know, Artie."

"Why don't you tell me something? Something about whatever interfered with my radar?"

Macintosh took another sip of his hot coffee. "I don't have any answers, but I know damn well it wasn't visitors from the stars."

"Probably not."

Macintosh choked on his coffee. "Probably!" he demanded incredulously. "You aren't seriously suggesting that Winkler's harebrained theory is right?"

"No, of course not. But I tell you, Mac, there's something very wrong about this whole thing. I've been working around radar my entire life, and I don't know of a single thing that could have produced these results. Do you have any leads?"

Macintosh frowned. What did he know? Really? He knew that the FBI suspected Lessing was involved in drug running and, since the unexplained lights had been spotted on Lessing's ranch, common sense suggested that Lessing's drug smuggling was tied to them. And more than likely so was the radar malfunction, but he couldn't prove it. What's more, he had his suspicions about Dr. Farron, who seemed to be right at home on Lessing's ranch. Suspicions that had escalated after she'd given him the slip when he'd tried to follow her out to the desert. Although it was possible that she hadn't realized he'd been behind her, he tried to be objective. She could just be such an appalling driver that she normally ran red lights.

"Mac?" Artie prodded.

"Sorry, I was thinking. I don't have any solid leads yet. Just suspicions. Check back with me in a few days and maybe I'll be able to tell you something then."

Artie got to his feet. "Will do. Just be careful you don't make yourself a target for Winkler."

"I'll be careful," Macintosh assured him. "I have no intention of making myself a target." For anyone, he thought, and that included an ingenious-seeming female and a dumb, blond male.

Five

"Jenna? Jenna?" Kynan's voice echoed through the house.

"I'm out here in the garage," she yelled, wondering what had distracted Kynan from his seemingly all-consuming task of constructing his transmitter.

The door leading into the kitchen opened, and Kynan stuck his head out. "What are you doing?" He came farther into the stifling heat of the garage and looked down at the broken bits and pieces of pottery scattered around her feet.

"Sorting what I found in the desert today." She stood and dusted the front of her white camp shirt. She'd much rather talk to Kynan than play with her finds.

"What's the problem?" she asked.

"You are out of ice cream."

"I can't be. There was a whole gallon of the stuff just a few days ago. Before you discovered it," she added thoughtfully.

"Is it rationed? Like on that documentary we saw about one of your eternal wars?"

"It wasn't wars they rationed," she said dryly. "It was the food for the hapless civilians. And no, ice cream is only rationed by sensible people concerned about their health."

"Their health?" Kynan looked confused. "I have health."

Jenna's eyes strayed down his magnificent body, lingering on his flat abdomen before continuing down the long, lean, length of his legs. The jade T-shirt he was wearing gave his skin a healthy glow and darkened his eyes almost to emerald. He certainly looked healthy, she conceded, but then looks could be deceptive. A tremor of uncertainty chased through her. And he had been through an awful lot recently.

"Kynan, what's your cholesterol level?"

"My what?"

"You know, the cholesterol level of your blood."

He shrugged. "I have no idea. Why would I?"

"Survival? It would be nice if you were to live to a ripe old age."

"Only if I manage to contact my fellow Atlanteans. About your lack of ice cream . . ."

"Easily solved. We'll go to the grocery store and buy some.

"And maybe we should get a few other chocolate things, like candy bars and cookies," Jenna added. Kynan had avidly devoured the brownies Mrs. Coltrain had given him last night when they'd visited her. In fact, he seemed to think chocolate was the epitome of gastronomical delights, and she vaguely remembered reading somewhere that chocolate produced the same reaction in the human body as did being in love.

Her eyes narrowed as the intoxicating idea of Kynan in love with her flittered through her mind, and a slow burning warmth sparked to life in her abdomen.

"Is going to the store a problem?" Kynan watched the emotions flit across her face.

"Um, no. I have more than enough money for the grocery store. But before we go, I want to ask Mrs. Coltrain if she needs anything."

"I'll go ask her," Kynan offered.

Jenna bit back her instinctive protest at letting him out of her sight. Protecting him was one thing. Smothering him was another. Kynan wasn't a stupid man. He wouldn't do anything to jeopardize his cover.

"Thank you," Jenna finally said. "While you do that, I'll pick up my things."

Kynan glanced down at them. "Have I used up all your space in the house?"

"No. I never keep my finds on the living-room floor. It's all yours."

Kynan gave her a long, thoughtful look, and then announced, "You are a very nice person, Jenna Farron. In fact—" he carefully stepped over the shards of pottery at her feet and cupped her chin in his large hand "—you are without a doubt the nicest person I have encountered."

Jenna ran the tip of her tongue over her dry lips as her gaze became entangled in the hot glow burning deep in his eyes. He definitely valued "nice," she thought distractedly as his face came closer and closer, filling her field of vision. His warm breath wafted across her cheeks, electrifying the hairs on her cheeks.

His mouth gently covered hers, and his lips felt hot. Hot and searching and infinitely exciting. His fingers curled around the back of her head, and he pulled her closer until her breasts brushed up against his chest. Pleasure shuddered through her.

Kynan's arms closed convulsively around Jenna, molding her pliant frame to him, and he pressed harder against her mouth. Her lips parted and his tongue accepted the unspoken invitation, surging inside to explore the dark warmth and sending a fizzling cascade of sensation along her nerve endings. Jenna reached up and ran her hand over his cheek, her fingertips lightly caressing his skin.

Long before she was ready to stop, Kynan raised his head and said, "I very much enjoy kissing you."

"Um, thank you," Jenna muttered, wishing she knew how his culture viewed sex or even kissing, for that matter. He'd complained about her culture being ambiguous on those subjects, but his own was a closed book to her.

"I enjoy kissing you, too," she said as she stepped back. "Now you go see Mrs. Coltrain, and I'll put my stuff up."

But instead of immediately moving her precious artifacts to safety, she leaned her forehead against the tiny window in the garage door and watched as Kynan crossed the street. An appreciative smile curved her lips at his brisk, purposeful stride. He didn't seem to do anything casually. What kind of lover would he be? Would he bring the same intensity to lovemaking that he brought to everything else he did? She shifted restlessly beneath the tantalizing images the thought provoked.

With a sigh of pure longing, she turned back to her artifacts.

Kynan returned ten minutes later—a thick slab of chocolate cake in one hand and a prescription Mrs. Coltrain needed filled in the other. Jenna shoved the prescription into her jeans pocket and, picking up her purse, climbed into the truck.

As soon as Kynan had polished off the last bite of cake and buckled his seat belt, Jenna opened the garage door and started the truck. She pulled to the end of the driveway and was in the process of checking both ways for cars, when she caught sight of a white car parked down the street in front of a vacant lot. She leaned over the steering wheel, trying to get a better look. It couldn't be Macintosh, she tried to tell herself. But she knew only too well that it could indeed.

"What's the matter?" Kynan asked.

"That white car about five houses down..." Jenna nodded toward it.

"The one with a man in it?"

"It's a man?" Jenna narrowed her eyes in an attempt to see behind the car's dark-tinted windshield, but in the twilight she couldn't.

"Yes," Kynan said slowly, "but I can't make out his features. You think it may be that army person who followed us the other day?"

"I'm afraid so. Damn!" she muttered in frustration. "Now what? We can't sit here at the end of the driveway or Macintosh will realize we're worried about him being there, and yet—"

She broke off as Kynan climbed out of the truck and, walking around to the right front, stared fixedly down at the wheel.

Jenna hastily shifted into Park and scrambled out after him.

"What are you doing?" she asked.

"Buying us time to consider a course of action. From what I've seen, none of your mechanical devices are very reliable, so he should find nothing suspicious about us inspecting the truck."

"Very clever." Jenna gave credit where it was due. "So what do we do? If we leave, Macintosh might break into the house and find all the stuff you're using to build the transmitter. But if we suddenly go back inside after seeing him, he'll be convinced we're trying to hide something.

"If I just knew whether Macintosh really knows anything about you or if he's just acting on a hunch." She chewed nervously on her lower lip.

"He can't know anything," Kynan said. "No one has found the suspension chamber, or the device I set up to record intruders would have alerted me."

Jenna took a deep breath. "All right, we'll assume he's just suspicious of us because he doesn't have anyone else to focus on. And he can't do much on just suspicions," she said, hoping it was true, but fearing it wasn't. From what she'd read lately, a lot of government agencies seemed to operate independently of either reason or the courts.

"Our best chance of escaping notice is to continue to behave in a normal manner," she said slowly.

"Oh. In that case, I can help."

Without any further explanation, Kynan enfolded her in his arms. Cradling her head against his shoulder, he began to kiss her with a great deal of enthusiasm.

What was he doing? The confused thought beat its way to the front of her mind only to sink beneath the weight of the emotions his mobile mouth was raising. She felt hot and prickly and antsy. And empty. Fantastic as his kisses were, they no longer satisfied her. She wanted more. Deliberately, she snuggled closer to him, fitting her curves against the much harder planes of his body.

His mouth wandered over her satiny skin, placing kisses along her jawline. Jenna shivered as a heavy, melting sensation flowed sluggishly through her veins.

"What are you...um..." Her shivers increased as he nibbled on her earlobe.

"Yes?" His voice had deepened perceptibly.

"Doing?" She forced the word out.

"Acting normally. Macintosh will think we're lovers."

"Macintosh should be convinced by now..." she muttered, fighting her way free of the maelstrom of desire in which she was drowning.

Kynan's tongue rubbed over her earlobe, and she jumped in reaction.

"I believe in doing a thorough job," he said.

"You get much more thorough and we'll find ourselves hauled in for indecent exposure." Determinedly, Jenna stepped away from him.

"Come on. Let's go get your ice cream." She clambered back into the truck. "You watch out the rearview mirror and see if Macintosh follows us."

She pulled out into the street, trying not to let her nervousness affect her driving.

"He's following," Kynan announced a few minutes later.

"Good. This trip should bore him and if he gets bored enough, maybe he'll go find someone else to hassle."

Five minutes later she pulled into the parking lot of the grocery store and cut the engine. She waited a few minutes until she saw Macintosh pull in at the other end of the lot.

"He'll probably wait here for us to finish. So let's hurry before he decides to go back to the house and snoop around."

Kynan followed her into the store, looking around curiously. "Where do they keep the ice cream?" he asked.

"Over there." Jenna pointed to the row of open freezers. "Here." She picked up a red plastic shopping basket and handed it to him. "Put your ice cream in this. I'm going to get Mrs. Coltrain's prescription filled. I'll meet you at the freezers."

Kynan nodded in agreement and with an anticipatory glint in his eye headed toward the middle of the store. Jenna, telling herself that he could hardly come to grief in the frozen food section, hurried toward the pharmacy at the back of the store. There were two other people waiting to pick up their prescriptions so she got in line. As she stood her gaze wandered absently only to be snagged by the colorful display beneath the counter.

Jenna's eyes narrowed slightly, and she furtively glanced over her shoulder. Kynan was nowhere to be seen. Satisfied, she began to study the variety of products, trying not to be obvious about it. Maybe she should buy a packet, she considered. She was certainly fascinated enough with Kynan to make love to him if she got the chance. And being a modern woman, it was up to her to make sure that there were no repercussions from it. Who knew what kind of birth control Kynan's people used. Or even if they did. No, it was up to her to take the initiative.

Her gaze wandered over the display consideringly. Flavored? she read with disbelief. How could you flavor latex? Condoms were made of latex, weren't they? She tried to remember what she'd read about them, but nothing specific came to mind. Her knowledge of birth control had been entirely theoretical up until now. She straightened her shoulders in determination. But that didn't mean she couldn't learn.

Jenna moved a step closer as the first person in line received her medicine and left. Neon? She read another label. Why neon? So you wouldn't lose the guy in the dark? She choked on a giggle she tried to suppress.

Size? Jenna suddenly realized that the blasted things came in sizes. How on earth was she supposed to know whether Kynan was small, medium or large. Compared to what? Her knowledge of male anatomy was sketchy, to say the least. He'd looked to be about the same size as the Michelangelo nudes she'd seen in Rome, but she had no idea what size models Michelangelo had favored. He could have had some preference to make his statues look better proportioned.

Jenna grimaced. There was a whole lot more to this protection business than one would think. She studied the well-stocked rows looking for a box of assorted sizes. She didn't find one, so she simply grabbed a box that looked promising and stood there, feeling as if everyone in the store were watching her.

When her turn came, she got Mrs. Coltrain's prescription and paid for the condoms. At least she didn't have to take them through the regular checkout line where Kynan would be sure to notice them. What would he think about her purchase? she wondered, as she shoved the small sack into her purse.

She had no idea. Not only did she have all the usual problems mentioned in the women's magazines about trying to communicate with a man, but the man with whom she was trying to communicate was ten thousand years behind the times.

Jenna rounded the end of the aisle and paused as she caught sight of Kynan leaning over the open freezer full of ice cream. Her eyes lingered on his absorbed expression as he studied the labels. He looked so endearingly earnest. She wanted to grab him and hug him. To press her mouth against the enticing tilt of his lips. To smooth back the golden lock of hair that had tumbled across his forehead. To... Jenna frowned as she suddenly noticed the woman at the other end of the freezer who was studying Kynan as if she couldn't believe her eyes. Or her luck. Jenna felt a shard of some dark emotion lacerate her composure. She didn't want another woman looking at Kynan like that. Kynan belonged to her.

No, she thought soberly. Kynan didn't belong to her. He belonged to himself.

She forced herself to watch as, with seeming casualness, the woman sidled closer to Kynan. In front of Jenna's outraged eyes, the woman leaned into the freezer, giving Kynan a better view of her well-developed cleavage.

There was no justice in the world, Jenna thought sourly. Why was it she'd gotten the well-developed mind and all society seemed to care about was a well-developed bust?

"I just don't know which flavor to buy." The woman's little-girl voice made Jenna want to gag. Talk about clichéd approaches!

"What do you think I should get?" The woman gave Kynan a melting glance.

Kynan straightened and looked at the woman as if noticing her for the first time. "If you have no idea what you want, how would you expect a stranger to be able to decide?" he asked.

"Haven't you heard that a stranger is just a friend you haven't met?" the woman tried.

"No," Kynan said simply.

The woman gave him a rueful grin. "Ah, well, you can't blame a girl for trying," she said as she moved off.

Kynan watched her go with a puzzled look on his face. A look that disappeared when he caught sight of Jenna.

"Come and see." He waved an expansive hand around the freezer. "I found eight varieties of chocolate."

Jenna ruthlessly stifled her impulse to ask him about the woman. She'd never had any patience with people who allowed jealousy to poison their relationships, but for the first time she had a clear idea what drove them. It was very hard to stand by and watch when someone tried to pick up a man with whom you were involved.

"Limit yourself to four. The freezer won't hold any more," she explained at his crestfallen expression.

"You need a bigger freezer," he complained.

"I have a bigger freezer. At home in Boston. This place is just a summer rental, and it came completely furnished."

Kynan wondered what kind of home Jenna had created for herself. She was such a captivating mixture. Not only was she the sexiest woman he'd ever encountered, but her sexiness was allied to a crystal-clear, sharp-edged mind and an emotional warmth that fascinated him. He didn't understand how such an imperfect world could have created such perfection.

Nor could he understand how she could function in this society. Although she did have Mrs. Coltrain to talk to and that bright young boy who brought her newspaper. Perhaps Jenna knew of other people like them in Boston. Maybe there were even more people like them here and she hadn't found them because they kept a low profile to avoid attracting the attention of the psychopaths who seemed to have free rein in this society. He didn't know. What he did know was that Jenna deserved better and wasn't going to get it on this planet. He also knew it was going to be hard to leave her when he made contact with his fellow Atlanteans.

"Chocolate Mocha's good." Jenna tried to hurry him along.

Kynan obediently tossed the flavor in, added three more, and then followed Jenna toward the checkout lanes.

Once they were outside, Jenna, after a quick glance to make sure that Macintosh was still there, headed toward the truck.

"We're in luck," she said. "He didn't sneak back to break into the house."

"I could rig a few electronic traps that would surprise an intruder," Kynan offered. While he didn't want to take time off from his work on the transmitter, if there was a possibility that Macintosh might try to break in...

Jenna considered the idea for a moment and then shook her head. "No, I don't think we should do anything that might draw attention to us. You go ahead and work on your transmitter."

Kynan took her at her word. For the next three days he spent his every waking minute trying to weld the various bits and pieces cannibalized from other machines into a transmitter with interstellar capabilities.

"I've been waiting for you." Kynan engulfed Jenna in a hug when she returned from the desert on the third night.

Jenna tilted her head back and looked up into his excited eyes. Her weariness seemed to drop away from her at Kynan's pleasure in seeing her. A sense of anticipation bubbled through her.

"Let me guess?" She grinned at him. "You've discovered a new flavor of ice cream?"

"Better than that." He dropped a quick kiss on her sun-warmed lips. "Hmm, you smell so good," he murmured as he nuzzled the soft skin beneath her ear. "Like sunshine and growing things..."

"And dust," Jenna said ruefully. "Tell me what happened while I get something cold to drink." She headed into the kitchen. "Macintosh hasn't been back, has he?"

"He drove by once that I saw, but forget him, he's not important." Kynan reached into the refrigerator and handed her an icy soft drink. "Come and see."

Clutching her can in one dusty hand, Jenna obediently followed him into the living room.

"There!" He gestured proudly toward the tiled area in front of the patio doors where a machine now stood in lonely splendor.

Jenna slowly circled the thing, trying to make head or tail of it. She couldn't. Of course, she probably wouldn't recognize a modern transmitting device, she conceded, let alone one jerry-built from the distant past.

"This, I take it, is your transmitter?" she said, torn between awe that he had actually managed to construct it out of spare parts, and sadness that his dream of contacting his compatriots was about to be proved a fruitless search. Poor Kynan. She winced at his happy expression. Reality was a hard taskmaster, and there wasn't a whole lot she could do to shield him from it. Sooner or later, he was going to have to face the truth. At least the delay had given him a chance to regain his strength.

"Yes." He ran his hand down one dull black side of the machine.

Like he was caressing a lover, Jenna thought as she watched his long fingers slide over the metal. What would it be like to have him caress her like that? Much as she'd like to find out, she didn't quite know how to move him from the enthusiastic kisses with which he greeted her to a more intimate stage, and she'd been leery of pushing him when he was so absorbed with building his transmitter. But now...

"Have you tried it out yet?" Jenna finally asked.

"No, I was waiting for you."

"Could you wait just a little longer while I wash away the part of the desert that's still clinging to me?" She rubbed her hands down the front of her dirt-streaked jeans.

"Sure. You do that while I check to make sure Macintosh hasn't returned."

Jenna shot the transmitter an apprehensive glance. "Don't tell me that this thing will interfere with radar like that machine in the cave."

"It will interfere with radar."

Jenna gave him a rueful grin. "I asked you not to tell me that."

"Do lies make the situation any more palatable?"

"It's said that ignorance is bliss."

"Not by me it isn't. But I'm just going to give it a short trial to test the crystals." For the first time, Kynan looked worried. "But I won't do it until he's gone."

"Fair enough," Jenna agreed and went to take her shower. She didn't like any of this. She didn't like Kynan's preoccupation with getting off the Earth. She didn't like Macintosh's preoccupation with watching them, and she most definitely didn't like her own growing preoccupation with Kynan. Taken together, they had the potential for disaster and she was the one sitting in the middle of the whole mess.

She knew full well that she was becoming far too involved with Kynan, but she didn't know what to do about it. She didn't seem to be able to maintain any kind of emotional distance. What was worse, she admitted honestly, she didn't really want to. Her feelings for him were so new that she didn't want to suppress them, she wanted to cherish them. And while her feelings were no problem at the moment, she knew she couldn't live her life in the present. The future had a nasty way of becoming the present just when you least wanted it.

She frowned as she remembered Macintosh. If he were to find out about Kynan, Kynan's future could consist of being little more than a state prisoner. Or worse. She shivered as she remembered a few of the more fanatical military types she'd encountered over the years. They could well demand that Kynan create some sophisticated killing machine for them. And he would refuse. She knew it in her heart.

Worry about one thing at a time, she told herself. And at the moment, making sure it was safe to test Kynan's transmitter was her first concern.

She hurried through her shower and then rushed back into the living room to find Kynan kneeling beside his creation. He was fiddling with something at its base.

Jenna automatically glanced toward the front door. "No Macintosh?"

"No," he said. "I looked up and down the street. No one is parked anywhere in sight. It's safe to try."

That was purely a matter of opinion, Jenna thought as she perched a safe distance away on the arm of the chair.

Kynan slowly got to his feet and leaned over the transmitter, pressing a lever at the base. His face was set in hard lines as if, by the very force of his concentration, he could compel it to function properly.

Jenna took a deep breath, trying to still her racing heart as she waited to see what would happen.

For a long moment, nothing did. But then she heard a faint humming noise coming from the machine. Unfortunately, the sound began to build, as did the pitch. Fearfully Jenna glanced at her windows. She didn't know if those commercials about high-pitched noise breaking glass were accurate or not, but she most emphatically didn't want to find out. Especially not in a rented house with Macintosh lurking somewhere in the background.

The sound continued to build until she could feel it vibrating in her teeth. She pressed her fingers in her ears, hoping that would help. It didn't. The sound grew steadily shriller, making her feel slightly frantic.

Kynan's lips were tightly compressed, and his hands clenched into fists.

Wasn't it supposed to sound like that? Jenna wondered. Kynan didn't look too happy about something.

Jenna gasped as the rising crescendo of noise reached a peak, sounding like a million fingers being simultaneously scraped across a blackboard. And then there was a second of abrupt silence. Overwhelming, all-consuming silence that was even more threatening than the noise, as if the whole world had paused, waiting for the final act.

It came in a spectacular burst. Brilliant, glittering sparks of color raced over the transmitter's dull black surface and dripped off onto the tile floor. It looked as if a rainbow had been broken into pinpoints of individually colored light, each one dancing over the machine.

Jenna looked from the scintillating display to Kynan's set face and realized that, beautiful as it was, it was defeat. Total and complete failure. And there wasn't a thing she could do to help. To lessen the blow. She watched as the cascading prism slowed and then faltered and finally died away into nothingness.

Kynan continued to stare helplessly at the machine, his shoulders bowed under the weight of his failure. Finally, he raised his head and turned toward her.

Jenna wanted to cry at the bleakness in his eyes. The sparkle was gone, replaced by a dullness that tore at her heart. She couldn't bear to see him so discouraged.

"Oh, Kynan," she muttered impotently.

She wrapped her arms around him and pressed herself against his chest. She could feel the heavy throbbing of his heart and the tremors shaking his overtense muscles.

"I'm sorry." She rubbed her hand over his cheek, trying to smooth out the lines carved there. "I'm so very sorry."

"I know, Jenna." He buried his face against her neck. "I can't bear..."

"It'll be all right." She murmured the soothing words with no other thought but to ease his grief, to replace his pain with something else. Instinctively, she placed a comforting kiss on his lips. It was like putting a match to tinder.

His arms tightened convulsively around her, and he shoved his fingers through her short hair, holding her head steady as his lips devoured hers. There was nothing comforting in his kiss. It reflected raw emotion backed by a raging, boundless need.

"Ah, my sweet Jenna." He lifted his head and stared down at her. "I want more from you than just kisses. I want.... But I don't know..."

"Know what?" Jenna asked.

"I can't get a clear reading on what your culture thinks about the physical act of love," he said in frustration. "The message seems to be very contradictory."

There was no contradiction about how she felt, Jenna thought. She wanted to make love to him. No ifs, ands or buts. Her hand strayed down to the pocket where she'd hidden a condom in the hope that this exact opportunity might arise.

"Jenna, is sex as prevalent as the television would lead one to believe?"

Jenna bit back her escalating sense of impatience. If Kynan needed to talk, then they'd talk even though she would far rather they explored the world of nonverbal communication.

"Well, it's hard to differentiate between what people really do and what they claim they do," she said, quoting a friend who taught in the psychology department.

"I don't care about people. I care about you. How often do you make love?" Kynan demanded.

Jenna winced at the bluntness of the question. Would Kynan think less of her because she'd never before made love to a man? Would he think the reason was because no one had ever found her desirable? For a moment Jenna toyed with the idea of simply lying, but she couldn't. Much as she craved making love to Kynan, the experience would be irrevocably tarnished if she lied to get him to agree. Kynan had to want her as she was, not as he thought she was.

She stared at the whitish button on his denim shirt, took a deep breath and said, "Actually... I've... never... made love to anyone." She finished in a rush.

"Why?"

"It's a long story," she muttered.

"Tell me," he ordered. "I want to understand."

She might as well tell him, she thought. If nothing else, it would distract him from his transmitter's failure.

"My parents never wanted children, and I was a midlife surprise," Jenna said, jumping into the middle of the story.

"They didn't want you?" Kynan's features tightened in outrage. "How could anyone not be overjoyed to have a child?"

"You'd be surprised," Jenna said sadly. "Anyway, they weren't sure what to do with me, so they hired a nanny and relegated me as a problem to be dealt with later."

"And?" he prodded when she fell silent.

"Later came when it became apparent that I was very bright. I was better off being ignored. At least my nannies let me do pretty much as I wanted. Once my parents got involved, it seemed as if my every waking moment was spent being tutored in something."

Kynan slowly stroked his hand over her short, silky hair, trying to soothe away the pain he could hear. "What about when you went to school?"

"It was worse. My parents insisted I be put in a class with kids studying at the same level as I was, instead of in a class with kids my own age. This meant that I was six years younger than my classmates. Socially, it was a disaster. Seventeen-year-old boys weren't the slightest bit interested in a kid of eleven. And by the time I was interested in boys I was working on a Ph.D. and the boys in my classes weren't boys, they were men. Men who had no interest in a shy, skinny teenager." She shrugged. "So, with one thing and another, I simply never... did.

"But that's not to say that I wouldn't like to, if you..." She couldn't quite get the rest of the words out.

"Oh, I most assuredly do want." The glow in Kynan's eyes intensified, and Jenna had the fanciful notion that if she were to hold out her hands she would be warmed in their reflected light.

"Why don't you take the lead? That way you can control the pace so you'll be comfortable," he suggested.

Comfortable? Jenna examined his word. She felt a lot of things when she was in Kynan's arms, but "comfortable" wasn't one of them. And what exactly was she supposed to do, anyway? she wondered nervously. How did one get from kissing to all the rest? For that matter, how did she go about getting her clothes off with any degree of sangfroid? Or his clothes? Her nerve quailed under the weight of all the things she didn't know.

"All right?" He gave her a tender smile that soothed her rising fears. His smile contained much more than sexual desire, Jenna realized. It held liking and respect for her as a person. She drew confidence from the knowledge.

"Yes." She tried to sound more assured than she felt.

"Good." Kynan dropped a quick kiss on her lips and then lowered himself onto the thick green shag rug. He leaned back and linked his hands together beneath his head. The movement pulled his blue knit shirt tightly across his chest, emphasizing his muscles.

Jenna studied him uncertainly as she tried to decide what to do. Where to start. Her eyes strayed the length of his body. Down over his chest, over his flat belly. Her breathing developed a catch to it when she saw the evidence of his arousal.

She peered up at his face through her thick, dark eyelashes. He was watching her with a warm, indulgent smile that made her feel cherished even if it didn't contain an answer to her present dilemma.

She was a bright, adaptable archaeologist, she encouraged herself. There was no reason why she shouldn't be just as good at making love to Kynan once she got the mechanics down. Maybe she could apply her knowledge of archaeology to making love? What if she were to think of him as an artifact she'd just found? A fascinating artifact that she wanted to know more about?

Dropping to her knees, Jenna reached out and placed her hands flat against his chest. The knit material of his shirt felt springy from the texture of his body hair beneath it. She flexed her fingers, digging the tips into his chest. His skin was warm and the muscles beneath it hard. It was an intriguing combination. Slowly, she rubbed her hands in ever-widening circles as she explored his exact dimensions.

If Kynan really were an artifact she'd found, the first thing she'd do would be to brush away the dirt covering him so that she could get a clear look at him. Not that he was covered with dirt, but his clothes did effectively conceal him. So she should get rid of them, she decided on a burst of bravado.

She grasped the bottom of his T-shirt and tugged it upward, over his chest and finally his head. Carelessly, she tossed it behind her, her attention on the thick layer of reddish-gold hair that covered his chest. She leaned forward and placed a light kiss in the exact middle of his breastbone. His hair felt infinitely exciting against her lips. She wanted to feel more. Much more.

She kissed him again, this time darting her tongue out to sneak a taste of his satiny skin. It was ever so faintly salty. Jenna breathed deeper, letting his unique scent flood her lungs. Dreamily, she dropped insubstantial kisses across one side of his chest, pausing to lightly flick her tongue over the tip of his flat nipple.

Kynan shuddered convulsively and, encouraged by his reaction, she began to paint erotic designs along his collar-bone with the tip of her tongue. His body went rigid and a feeling of power welled within her, feeding her desire and making her bolder. Making love wasn't hard at all, she thought in triumph.

Her gaze drifted lower, coming to rest on his silver belt buckle. A good archaeologist needed to uncover the entire specimen before she became too engrossed with any one part of it.

She reached for his belt with fingers made clumsy by a heady combination of desire, anticipation and lingering shyness. Finally worrying the buckle free, she unzipped his jeans. Grasping the waistband, she tugged down both his pants and shorts.

Kynan helpfully lifted his hips and quickly kicked out of them.

Jenna's eyes widened at the sight of his masculinity and a stab of longing slashed through her.

Her gaze returned to Kynan's face. His narrowed-eyed intensity made her feel like the most important thing in the world to him. Her sense of confidence escalated, and she trailed her fingertips down over his flat belly, tentatively stroking the hot length of him. His flesh seemed to burn her skin.

"Jenna!" He caught her hand and moved it away. "I know I said I'd let you... but... I don't think I can wait." He took a deep breath and the ribs in his chest expanded beneath her fascinated eyes. "If I don't get to kiss you now..." He grabbed her wrist and tugged her forward.

Caught off guard, Jenna fell across his bare body. The musky scent of his skin engulfed her, seeming to isolate them in their own little world. A world she'd been waiting for her whole life and she hadn't even known it.

"Ah, my darling Jenna." Kynan's warm breath lifted the silky hair around her face. "I want so much..." He grasped the back of her neck and pulled her lips down to meet his. They were hot, and searching. Tension began to twist in her abdomen, and Jenna squeezed her eyes together to better focus on it.

"You taste delicious," he muttered as his tongue stroked over her lower lip. "But you have too many clothes on."

Jenna raised her head and stared down at him, trying to process his words through the desire muddling her thoughts. *Clothes.* She latched on to the word. Kynan thought she had too many clothes on. But would he find her body as fascinating as she found his? She wasn't very voluptuous. In fact, she wasn't the least bit voluptuous. Would he find her a disappointment? She looked down into his eyes. The blue was entirely gone. They were a bright, clear green. Like spring grass. Like new beginnings.

Taking a deep breath, she pulled her T-shirt off and tossed it onto the couch. It took a minute for her to find the courage to look at Kynan. He was staring at her lace-covered breasts as if mesmerized by the sight. Reaching out, he lightly brushed his fingers over the tips of her breasts. Jenna swallowed as they convulsed in reaction, their tips becoming turgid buds of desire.

He didn't look disappointed. The obvious truth encouraged her to unfasten her bra, letting it fall to the floor.

The blaze in his eyes increased, becoming a raging inferno of desire. Desire for her, Jenna thought wonderingly. There was no way Kynan could be faking his reaction. No reason for him to. He wanted her. Badly. Feeling greatly daring, she rocked forward and brushed the tips of her breasts against his chest. His hair scraped abrasively against the sensitive points, and she trembled beneath the torrent of sensation that poured through her.

Kynan took her in his arms and rolled over, crouching above her. His wide frame filled her vision, making her feel protected from the outside world.

His fingers fumbled with the zipper on her jeans. As he pulled them off, she suddenly remembered something.

"Um, Kynan..."

Kynan dropped a kiss on the end of her nose and then ran his lips over her left eyebrow. "Yes, my precious one?"

She fumbled for her jeans and pulled out the foil-wrapped packet. "This is... I..." She ground to a stop. Unfortunately, there was nothing in archaeology that even vaguely compared to this situation.

Kynan took the packet from her unresisting fingers. "For me?" he said.

"Um, well, yes, in a manner of speaking. You see...it's protection."

Kynan looked around the room in confusion. "From what?"

Jenna took a deep breath and blurted out, "Unplanned pregnancies."

Kynan opened the package and studied it curiously. "Interesting..." he muttered. "But not very efficient."

Kynan placed the packet within easy reach and lowered his head. The lingering kisses he placed over her face brought a shimmer of heat to her skin. Jenna shifted restlessly, wanting something more substantial than these teasing kisses. Something far more substantial.

At long last, Kynan reached her mouth, and her lips eagerly parted to admit his hot, seeking tongue. Desire ricocheted through her, building in intensity until its constant throbbing blotted out rational thought.

The throbbing increased to a fever pitch as his hand slipped between her legs and his finger gently rubbed over the core of her femininity.

Jenna gasped at the explosive feeling that spiraled through her. Mindlessly, she raised her hips against his caressing hand and a low moan escaped from between her clenched teeth.

"Please," she muttered, not even sure exactly what she was asking for. She just knew there had to be more. The exquisite feeling had to lead to something else. Something the scope of which she could only dimly perceive.

Kynan slipped between her legs. His thighs were hard and felt like rasped silk against her much softer skin. The difference between them increased her sense of excitement.

He carefully positioned himself against her moist flesh and, cupping her face in his hands, took her mouth in a deep, searching kiss. At the same moment, he surged forward, filling her.

Jenna tensed as her body struggled to accommodate his masculine intrusion.

"Slowly, go slowly," Kynan muttered against her mouth and Jenna wasn't sure if he was talking to himself or to her. Nor did she care. She didn't care about anything except the feeling that had wrapped itself around her and was squeezing out all of her inhibitions. A feeling of frantic desperation began to grow as Kynan moved back and forth with gathering speed. It seemed as if each of his thrusts intensified the feeling, until her body could no longer contain it. The slender thread holding her tethered to reality finally snapped, hurtling her into a seemingly endless void filled with sparkling warmth and frenzied excitement.

It had been worth waiting for the right man, Jenna thought wonderingly, holding Kynan tightly as his body convulsed in its own release. And to think that she could feel this way again and again.... The future seemed painted in shades of pure promise as she closed her eyes and allowed exhaustion to overtake her.

Six

Jenna looked up from the archaeological notes she was pretending to read and glanced over at Kynan, sitting in the middle of the living-room floor amid the dismantled components of his burned-out transmitter. She watched as he made a notation on the pad of paper at his feet before lapsing back into his thoughts.

Blast that transmitter, anyway! Who cared if Kynan ever got it to work after its spectacular fizzle yesterday. She certainly didn't. There were so many more interesting things they could be doing. A flush skated along her cheekbones as the memory of their lovemaking popped into her mind. As it did every time she allowed her mind to wander. Probably because she wanted to do it again. And again. A soft, soundless sigh escaped her as she continued her study.

Kynan's lips were pressed together, either in concentration or worry. Or, quite possibly, both. All she knew for certain was that she wanted to kiss them. To explore their exact texture. To savor the taste of them.

But what did Kynan want? Much as she craved his love-making, she wanted him to want it, too, and at the moment appeared that the only thing he wanted was to work on his transmitter.

Discouraged, she propped her chin in her hand and considered the situation. She could always try seducing him. But in order to seduce him, she'd first have to get his attention and she had the disheartening feeling that, given his present state of preoccupation, he wouldn't notice her unless she somehow managed to transmit radio waves. But she could wait, she encouraged herself. Kynan was a very intelligent man. Sooner or later, he'd face the fact that he wasn't going to be able to contact anyone, no matter what the state of his transmitter. And when he did, she'd be here.

But would Kynan be here? Her feeling of anticipation faded as she remembered her fears about what Macintosh would do if he found out about Kynan.

A sense of panic filled her at the thought of not being able to see Kynan whenever she wanted. To talk to him. To make love to him.

Maybe it would be better to take the initiative away from Macintosh, Jenna considered. Maybe Kynan should tell his story to one of the television newsmagazines. That way, the government wouldn't be able to hide Kynan away somewhere and try to pretend he didn't exist. Not after a few million people had heard him. And seen him. Her eyes lingered on his golden hair.

Kynan would be a monster hit with the media. He'd probably have a fan club within a week. A dark spurt of jealousy oozed through Jenna. She didn't want a bunch of women with more hormones than brains lusting after him. Jenna's unsettled feeling deepened as she realized that a lot of very intelligent, very self-possessed women also would be clamoring to talk to him. To try to wring information about Atlantis out of him. The thought made her shift unhappily.

"Yes."

She glanced up at Kynan's muttered word, only too eager to abandon a subject she found upsetting in the extreme.

"Yes what?"

Kynan gestured toward the plate on the coffee table containing the shards of crystal that had splintered when the transmitter blew. "Yes, I have a solution for them."

Jenna studied the shattered bits for a long moment. "Glue?"

"A substitute. A substance with enough of the same properties as the original crystals so that it should work well enough to transmit my message. At least, it will work if I can get it shaped the way I need it." For a moment doubt shadowed his eyes.

"What is the substance?"

"Just a diamond."

"'Just' and 'diamonds' don't go together," she said dryly. "Try diamonds and exclamation points."

Kynan looked uncertain. "Diamonds have always been relatively common in the Earth's crust."

"So has man's greed for them."

Kynan ran his fingers through his hair. "I must get one," he insisted. "Without a diamond, the transmitter won't work."

"How about more of those crystals?" Jenna nodded toward the coffee table.

"They'd be better," he conceded. "But I don't have any more."

"What about taking some out of that big machine in the cave?"

"The crystals in it are sealed into the power source. If I had the equipment to cut through the seal, I would also have the means to cut my own crystals."

Jenna sighed. "Classic catch-22. Then I guess it's a diamond."

"You'll help me?"

Jenna looked into his hopeful eyes and felt her heart twist strangely. Yes, she thought. She'd help him. And not just because she liked him very, very much, but also because she respected him as a fellow scientist. "Of course, I'll help. Do you have any idea what size diamond you need?"

Kynan handed her a detailed drawing showing the precise size and angle of the faceting. "It has to match this exactly in order to transmit the signal."

Jenna whistled. "Elizabeth Taylor should have been the one to find you." She stared out through the sliding-glass patio doors at the rosebushes lining the rock wall at the back of the yard.

"I think our best bet would be to try and buy this through a friend of mine from the university. His name is John Warton, the head of my department. He's an expert on ancient jewelry. What he doesn't know about cut stones isn't worth knowing. May I mark on this?" She gestured with the drawing.

"Sure." Kynan watched as she scribbled a note to John, explaining what they wanted.

"How long will it take to get an answer?" Kynan watched curiously as she activated the fax machine in the corner.

Jenna shrugged. "It depends. If John is in his office and has time to chase down the facts right away, we could have a response this afternoon. If not, hopefully by tomorrow."

"Tomorrow!"

"Rome wasn't built in a day. John'll get back to me as soon as he can."

Kynan sighed. "If you say so. I think I'll go over and see Mrs. Coltrain. She has an idea for a cat door she wants me to install."

"I'll help." Jenna tossed aside her notebook. She would much rather spend the time with Kynan than work on her notes.

* * *

"Hey, Mac." Artie stuck his head into Macintosh's small office. "I've been looking all over for you."

Macintosh looked up. "You found me, so have a seat and tell me what you want." He waved toward the chair in front of his desk.

"Have you found out anything more about either those lights or my radar malfunction?" Artie asked.

"No, but the further I dig, the more I am convinced that drug smuggling is behind it. And I'm also beginning to think that Jenna Farron is in up to her neck."

Artie rubbed the side of his jaw thoughtfully. "So who's Jenna Farron?"

"Her cover is that she's an archaeologist. Which gives her an impeccable excuse to be wandering around in the desert without anyone thinking a thing about it."

"Convenient. But why do you suspect her?"

Macintosh shrugged. "It makes sense, given what I know."

"Which is?"

"One—" Macintosh began to tick points off on his fingers "—I know that Lessing supposedly has ties to a Colombian drug cartel. Two, I've found out that Lessing has never ever allowed anyone on his property before, *for any reason*. But suddenly out of the clear blue sky, he lets this Jenna Farron go wandering over it. Why? The only reason I can think of is that she's a contact from the person he and the cartel are selling the drugs to. I think she's here to make sure there's no slipups. Third, I followed her to the store one evening and, when she went inside, I tried to get a look in her truck."

"And?" Artie prodded.

"And I could see a residue of whitish powder in the bed of the truck."

"Cocaine?" Artie asked in excitement.

"I think so, but before I could get a sample for analysis, she came out and I had to retreat.

"And finally, she acts..." He gestured inarticulately. "Nervous," he finally said.

"Hell, man, if you treated the woman to your patented imitation of Torquemada, it's no wonder she acted frightened!"

"No," Macintosh said slowly. "I don't think she's afraid of me. Not exactly. And there's one final thing that nails it as far as I'm concerned. She's got a guy named Anderson staying with her. And according to her neighbors that I talked to, he showed up immediately after the radar interference.

"My gut feeling is that the drug cartel wiped out our radar with some kind of machine that reflects blue lights when it's used, then flew a shipment into Lessing's ranch and this Anderson came with it to supervise the operation."

"It does seem to be one coincidence too many that Anderson would appear immediately on the heels of the radar disturbance," Artie agreed.

"I'll tell you another reason I think he's an illegal alien who flew in with the shipment. Farron doesn't let him talk. It's like she's afraid he'll give away his background if he says very much."

Artie laughed. "Maybe. And maybe this Farron is a radical member of the women's movement, and views Anderson as just a dumb sex object."

Macintosh frowned as he remembered the man's eyes. They'd sparkled with intelligence and something else. Something he couldn't quite put a name to. No, whatever that man was, he wasn't stupid. "She says he's a visiting professor from Sweden."

"Which would neatly explain his lack of familiarity with American customs." Artie picked up on the point. "What does he look like?"

"Tall, muscular, with golden-blond hair one almost never sees these days."

"Perhaps not in this country, but when was the last time you were in Sweden? Do you have any solid facts about Farron?"

Macintosh gestured toward the papers on his desk. "These came in from Washington this afternoon in response to my request for information."

Artie picked one up and glanced over it. "According to this, she really is an archaeologist, and she really does teach at the university."

"No, Jenna Farron is an archaeologist, and Jenna Farron teaches at a university."

"You think this woman did away with the real Jenna Farron and took her place?"

"Not really. If she is an impostor, it's far more likely that she simply showed up in El Paso claiming to be Jenna Farron. Think about it. It's summer, so Farron's not at the university. She could be anywhere. No one would know the difference.

"It's also possible that she really is Jenna Farron and is simply picking up some money over the summer running drugs. Hell, we've got top-ranking government officials advocating legalizing drugs, why not a college professor?"

Artie nodded. "As you say, any of those scenarios are possible, but proving them could be a real problem. Are you going to ask Defton for more help?"

"Not yet, and I'd appreciate it if you didn't say anything to him, either. I want some proof before I go to him," Macintosh hedged, knowing that if Defton found out what he'd discovered, he'd be ordered to dump the whole thing in the FBI's lap.

"Of course I won't say anything, but if I can help out in any way, just yell. I don't have all that much to do right now, which reminds me why I came in the first place. I wanted to know if you'd fill in for Bert on our bowling team tonight. He's down with the flu."

Bowling! Macintosh's chest twitched in pain at the very thought of trying to throw a sixteen-pound ball down an alley.

"Sorry," Macintosh lied. "Much as I'd like to help, I'm waiting for the head of Dr. Farron's department at the university to return my call. Since there wasn't a picture in any of the stuff that came from Washington, I thought he might be able to tell me if Dr. Farron really is in El Paso."

"Too bad," Artie said. "Maybe another time."

"Maybe," Macintosh echoed as he watched him leave. And maybe not. Not if the Army had its way. Who knew where he'd end up if they discharged him. He'd spent his entire adult life in the Army. He had no family left. No friends outside the military. He'd never even owned a house.

A feeling of desolation swept over him. He couldn't let them discharge him. He'd have nothing. Nothing and no one and no place. It would be as if he didn't exist. The pain in his chest began to escalate as his agitated feelings made his heart pound.

The phone rang, providing a welcome distraction, and he grabbed it. "Colonel Macintosh here."

"This is Dr. John Warton's office returning your call, Colonel."

"Is Dr. Warton there?"

"No, sir. He had to leave to check something for a colleague, but he asked me to get back with you and find out what it was you needed. I'm Susan Woodrow, the departmental secretary," the woman added.

Macintosh bit back an exclamation of annoyance. He wanted to talk to the man in charge, not some secretary. Although…maybe it was better this way. A secretary would have no reason to lie to him. But if this Warton realized that the Army suspected one of his professors of drug smuggling, he'd undoubtedly lie to protect her. In his experience, college professors were all a bunch of anarchists.

"I'm trying to locate Dr. Farron, whom I believe is with your department."

"Yes, she is, but I'm afraid that she's not at the university this summer. She's doing fieldwork down by the Mexican border near El Paso," Susan said.

"What does Dr. Farron look like?"

"Just what is the problem, sir?" Susan sounded suspicious.

"Just a routine investigation. We like to keep track of the people working near our high-clearance facilities, and we think she may have inadvertently wandered onto our base," Macintosh replied, spinning a plausible lie. "If the woman in question really is Dr. Farron, then of course we don't have to worry, but since we don't know what she looks like..."

"She has black eyes, short black hair, is about five-four, very slender and very pretty.

"She's also very nice. You certainly don't have to worry about Dr. Farron," Susan said emphatically. "We think a lot of her here at the university. In fact, that's why Dr. Warton isn't here to talk to you himself. He went to find out how much that diamond she asked about costs."

"Diamond?" Macintosh tried to ignore the spurt of excitement that constricted his breathing. Was she trying to convert the proceeds from her smuggling to something more portable than cash?

"That's what I said." The edge in Susan's voice became more pronounced. "I think if you have any more questions you should wait and talk to Dr. Warton."

"But—" Macintosh began, only to stop when he realized that he was talking to a dead connection. He'd found out plenty and it all fit. That woman really was Dr. Farron, and she and Anderson were undoubtedly smuggling. And very profitably, too, if they were buying diamonds. Now all he had to do was prove it. And fast. Time was running out for him.

He glanced out the window at the bright afternoon sunlight. He'd wait until dusk and then go over and watch Farron's house for a while. Maybe something would happen. Something he could use against them.

"Yes, sir." Jenna dutifully chuckled at Dr. Warton's joke even though she felt more like crying. She'd been afraid the news would be bad when it had taken John two days to return her call. "I'll let you know." She carefully hung up the phone and reluctantly turned to the eagerly waiting Kynan.

"Well?" he demanded. "What did he say about my diamond?"

Jenna grimaced. "This has to be the classic case of 'I have good news and bad news.' It seems that getting the diamond itself presents no problem. Dr. Warton knows two sources that can have the diamond cut to your specifications an hour after you order it."

"Perfect." Kynan's eyes gleamed with relief.

"Not quite. There is the question of where do we get the $103,000 that we need to pay for it."

Kynan looked confused. "That's a problem?"

"You'd better believe that's a problem," she said dryly. "Universities are not known for paying their professors large salaries. Even if I were to liquidate everything I own I couldn't raise that much. And no one in their right mind would loan that amount to me on a teacher's salary."

Kynan leaned back in his chair and stared at the ceiling. "There has to be a way."

Drawn to him by a force she didn't understand and couldn't resist, Jenna walked over to him.

Kynan reached out and gathered her into his lap.

Happily, Jenna snuggled against his chest.

"It's very illogical," he murmured. His breath stirred her hair and tickled her ear. "But I think better when I'm holding you."

"You do?"

"Yes." He looked down into her gleaming black eyes and felt a curious twisting sensation in his gut. His intense reaction to her didn't make a great deal of sense. He'd known many women in his time. Some had been friends, some colleagues, and some he'd shared emotional relationships with, but none of them had touched him in quite the same way Jenna did, or as deeply. Jenna Farron had infiltrated the very essence of his being. She was fast becoming a necessary component of his life.

What was going to happen when he left Earth? Would he forget her when she wasn't there? *No.* He answered his own question. Jenna was far too vibrant a personality to simply be forgotten.

Maybe he could take her with him. He weighed the idea. With her quick mind and well-developed ethics, she'd be far more at home in the world he was seeking than the one into which she'd been born. But would she want to come? The question nagged at him. Despite the fact that she seemed to be all too aware of her culture's shortcomings, she inexplicably seemed to like it.

And that wasn't his only problem, he conceded. There was also the question of just how deep her feelings for him went. She'd made love to him with a fervor that in his world would have signified a commitment, but here . . . He felt a jab of frustration. He just didn't know, and he was afraid to ask her—for the simple reason that he might not like the answer. All he could do was continue to strengthen the bond between them and hope that when the time came to leave, she would choose to go with him.

His eyes lingered on the bluish gleam of her night-dark hair. "And I think even better when I'm kissing you," he murmured.

Strange, Jenna thought distractedly. When Kynan kissed her, she ceased to think at all and simply felt. She focused on his lips. They were such perfect lips. Not too thin and not too full, firm and warm and infinitely exciting.

Jenna's gaze traveled upward to be snared by the blaze of desire that had leached the blue out of his eyes. And she was the one responsible for it. The knowledge fed her self-confidence.

"Far be it from me to stifle anyone's creative processes," she told him.

"In that case..." Kynan kissed her with a hunger he made no attempt to hide. He wanted her. His craving was an almost-tangible entity vibrating between them.

For a few moments, he was content to merely savor the taste of her lips. Then, suddenly, it wasn't enough. He wanted more. He needed more. He shoved his fingers through her silky hair, holding her still as he lightly traced the outline of her lips with the tip of his tongue.

When Jenna's lips parted, he pushed his tongue inside and a shudder racked him at her exquisite taste. Slowly, prolonging the sensation, he stroked his tongue over the velvety inside of her cheek.

He could feel the tiny tremors that vibrated through her. She was so perfect. So absolutely perfect. He lifted his hand and reverently brushed his fingertips over the side of her cheek. Her skin was soft and velvety, like the petals on the roses in the backyard. She was very much like a rose. *Delicately beautiful and intoxicatingly fragrant,* the disjointed thought floated through his mind. But she was so much more. His hand slipped down to her breast and his fingers cupped her sensitive flesh.

The frantic beating of her heart against his palm excited him. He wanted to make love to her. To carry her into the bedroom and make long, slow, delicious love to her. To pleasure her in a million different ways while he indulged his own senses. *But this wasn't the time.* He clamped down on his escalating desire with a monumental effort. They had a problem now. A problem he needed to solve if they had any hope of getting off this misbegotten world.

Kynan raised his head and stared down into Jenna's eyes. They were huge. Dark with misty, unfocused depths that sent a shiver of longing vibrating through him. She looked...

Kynan blinked as he suddenly remembered something. The unfocused quality of Jenna's eyes was very similar to that of the woman on the television talk show he'd seen yesterday. She had been trying to explain the compulsive lure of gambling.

"Bingo!" he said.

"I'll say," Jenna muttered.

"Can we get enough?"

She could never get enough, Jenna thought dreamily. Not even if the two of them found themselves a deserted island and did nothing but make love for the next forty years.

"That Indian reservation advertises on television," he said thoughtfully.

Indian reservation? The phrase pricked the cocoon of sensual euphoria that held Jenna in thrall. She blinked, mentally scrambling to adjust her mind to reality. It wasn't easy. She much preferred the world of her senses to the everyday world with its myriad assortment of problems.

She leaned back and the space between them helped her somewhat. "What advertisement?"

"For high-stakes bingo," he explained. "We'll get the money for the diamond by winning it."

Jenna stared out the patio window as she considered his unorthodox idea for fund-raising. As a method of finance it left a lot to be desired. "Our chances of winning are not good," she argued. "The house normally wins or they wouldn't be able to stay in business."

"Yes, but we have something in the hole."

"Something... You mean an ace in the hole? What? Our sterling characters?" she asked dryly.

"This." Kynan reached into the neckline of his T-shirt and pulled out the intricately carved crystal.

Jenna glanced at it, immediately experiencing the weird tug at her senses she always felt when she looked directly at it. She hastily looked away.

"How can that help?" she asked curiously.

"I can use it to physically affect the movement of objects. And from what they said on the show on gambling, bingo is determined by which balls come up. So if I were to pick the balls..."

Jenna chewed on her lower lip as she weighed the ethics of the situation. They were abysmal. On the other hand, so was Kynan's need. Did she have the right to try and talk him out of something that he needed to preserve his sanity? Could she? Her eyes traced over the lean planes of his face. Probably not. And if she refused to help, he might well try to do it himself. With disastrous results. She shivered at the thought of what might happen if he got caught.

"From what distance does that work?" Jenna asked.

"A maximum of twelve feet from the object you want to control."

"Forget bingo," she said. "You wouldn't be able to get that close to the machine that picks the balls."

"Oh." He looked crestfallen.

"But there's always Las Vegas," she said. "We could get close enough to the dice games or the roulette wheel to influence it. And, I'd much rather take a bunch of professional gamblers for the money than the Indians."

"Fine." Kynan tipped her out of his lap and stood. "Let's go."

"No, let's plan first," Jenna said. "Plane tickets should be easy enough to get. Those I can afford, but there's the problem of our personal shadow." She cautiously opened the front door a crack and peered down the street.

"He's not there. Maybe he gave up," she said hopefully.

"Maybe." Kynan's doubts were evident in his voice. "But whatever his motivation, we ought to take advantage of his absence and go."

Jenna closed the door. "If Macintosh should follow us to Vegas, would he be able to detect you using that thing?"

Kynan shook his head. "No. Even in my time, the only device capable of picking up the expanded brain waves created by its use were huge stationary machines. Your culture has nothing to compare to that, let alone a portable model."

"That's one point in our favor," she said. "I'll call a travel agency about the tickets and you start to pack. With luck we can be out of here within the hour."

Unfortunately Lady Luck turned a deaf ear to Jenna's hopes. There were no vacant seats on any of the planes to Las Vegas until early the next morning. Having no alternative but to accept the delay, Jenna made the bookings and then settled down to wait. It was not an easy task.

Kynan paced. Back and forth across the living room he went, reminding Jenna of a tiger she'd once watched at the zoo. Kynan had the same supple fluidity of movement and the same barely concealed impatience. He needed something to distract him.

Her wandering gaze lit on the television.

Picking up the remote control, she turned it on. She flipped through the channels until she found a science documentary that looked as though it might interest Kynan.

"What's that?" Kynan stopped pacing and looked at the screen.

"It's an enlargement of a common-cold virus."

As she'd hoped, Kynan sat down beside her and studied the picture. "That looks like a pretty basic virus to me," he said.

"You had viruses in Atlantis?"

"Sure. It's been theorized that they're the oldest living things on earth."

"I don't care how long it's been living, I just wish they could kill it," she said.

Kynan looked surprised. "You can't?"

"No. Could your culture?"

"We could kill viruses of any sort, so I assume this one wouldn't present much of a problem."

Jenna stared at him in shock. "How?" she demanded.

Kynan shrugged. "That isn't my field of expertise."

"But could you take the knowledge your culture had and use it today?" she persisted.

"Probably. But all the medical information was stored with the people at Aix-al-Chin."

"Wait a minute. You mean you weren't the only one put in suspended animation?"

"Of course not. The engineering repository was actually a very minor site. The big ones were the medical facility, the agricultural station and the historical archives."

"Historical archives?" Jenna swallowed. For the first time in her life she truly understood the phrase, "drooled in anticipation." To actually get her hands on Atlantis's records would be mind-boggling. Not only could she indulge her love of the past to the fullest, but Kynan could use the information stored at the sites to bargain for his freedom with the government.

Although . . . Ugly reality put a brake on her enthusiasm. Considering the potency of some of Kynan's devices she had seen so far, she wouldn't trust any government to use them. They could too easily fall into the wrong hands, and the very thought of some of his machines at the disposal of an extremist group . . .

Jenna shivered. Any information leaked into her culture from Kynan's would have to be carefully controlled.

"But at least one of those sites should have operated as planned." Kynan further dashed her hopes. "And if one did, then they would have revived the others and removed the information stored there."

"They didn't revive you." Jenna was quick to point out the flaw in his argument.

"True," Kynan conceded. "And they should have. My site controlled the machines, and they would have needed the machines to refound society. I wonder what did happen?"

"Do you know where the other sites are?"

"Only in a very general sense," he said. "To actually locate them, I'd need a specialized homing device."

"Which you don't have?" Jenna guessed.

"No, unfortunately the one at my site malfunctioned."

It might be possible to go looking for them, Jenna considered. Her being an archaeologist would be the perfect cover for them. Maybe next summer when Kynan had accepted the fact that there weren't any survivors for him to contact...

She jumped as the front doorbell rang. Was the colonel back? Again? She glanced nervously at the piles of parts littering the floor, all connected to Kynan's transmitter. Hastily, she jumped to her feet and closed the curtains on the sliding-glass doors.

"We'd better answer it," Kynan said. "If it is Macintosh, not answering will only increase his suspicions."

Taking a deep breath, Jenna hurried to the front door and, flipping on the porch light, peeked out through the spy hole. "It isn't Macintosh. It's someone wearing a brown uniform."

"Military?" Kynan whispered.

"Not one of ours and Mexico's military would hardly be running around El Paso, ringing doorbells." She opened the door and peered out at the man, relaxing as she saw the insignia of the electric company on his shirt pocket.

"Is there a problem with the electricity?" she asked.

The man heaved a dispirited sigh. "No, ma'am. The problem is with the flu. We're really shorthanded this week, and I still have to read the meters on this street before I can all it a night. I just wanted to let you know I was here so you wouldn't think I was an intruder and call the cops."

"Thank you." Jenna's warm smile reflected her sense of relief. This man was no threat to anything but her budget.

"Uh, ma'am, would you happen to know where the meter is? This isn't my regular route."

"Sure. Come on. I'll show you," Jenna offered in the hopes of speeding him on his way. She led the man around to the back of the house with Kynan bringing up the rear.

"There you are." She gestured to the meter to the right of the patio doors, mentally congratulating herself for having had the foresight to pull the curtains. A meter reader probably wouldn't know what Kynan's bits and pieces were, but he might mention it to someone. And with Macintosh snooping around, who knew where that might lead.

"Thanks, ma'am." The man squinted at the meter, trying to read it. "Sir, could you give me a hand?" He pulled a flashlight out of his pocket, flipped it on and handed it to Kynan. "Just focus it on the front of the meter."

Kynan did and the man quickly jotted down some numbers in the book he was carrying.

"Thanks a lot, folks." He shoved the notepad in his pocket and took the flashlight back from Kynan. "Have a nice evening," he said as he left.

Kynan reached out and slowly pulled Jenna into his arms. "Actually," he murmured, "I plan on having a fantastic night."

Jenna took a deep breath to still her suddenly racing heart and snuggled closer. "Really?" She smiled seductively at him. "Do tell me more."

"Better still, I'll show you." He urged her toward the door, and Jenna went on a tide of rising excitement.

"Did you get it?" Macintosh demanded, the minute the meter reader reached the white car parked around the corner.

"Yeah. Here you are, Colonel." The man carefully dropped the flashlight he was holding into the plastic bag Macintosh held open. "There should be a clear set of the man's prints on it. What'd he do, anyway?"

"Just a routine investigation." Macintosh gave the stock answer. "Thanks for your cooperation."

"Always glad to help the military." The man pocketed the bill Macintosh handed him and left.

Sure, for a price, Macintosh thought grimly. But it didn't matter. He gently placed the bag with the flashlight in it on the front seat of his car. He'd send those prints off to Washington and with any luck he'd find out exactly who Jenna Farron's accomplice was. And then he'd make his move.

Seven

—

"If I could just figure out how to generate this kind of interest in my students, there's no telling what I could teach them." Jenna glanced around the crowded Las Vegas casino. It was packed with gamblers of all ages and sizes, from the businessman in a hand-tailored suit playing blackjack to a garishly dressed senior citizen methodically feeding coins into a slot machine.

Kynan winced as the din beat against his eardrums. He didn't like this. There were too many people. But he was here for a purpose, he reminded himself. And if he failed in his purpose, then he was trapped in this world for the rest of his natural life. The horrendous thought gave him the courage to follow Jenna as she wove her way through the throng.

She paused beside the craps table. "This is the game we want," she whispered in his ear.

"Here." Jenna shoved the pile of chips they'd purchased from the casino at him.

"Good luck." She impulsively placed a quick kiss on his lips.

"Hey, lady, you passing out good-luck charms to just anybody or do we have to pay?" A bleary-eyed man standing on the other side of Kynan leered suggestively.

Jenna opened her mouth to annihilate him but before she could, the man seemed to trip over his own feet—while standing absolutely still—and fell, landing on the floor with a thump.

Jenna shot a quick glance at Kynan, almost giggling at his smug expression. Instinctively her gaze dropped to the slight bump in the front of his tan twill shirt where she knew the crystal was nestled. She absolutely had to get one of those things. They would make the mace industry obsolete.

"Forget our inebriated friend and concentrate on the game." She dragged her mind back to the problem at hand. "We need to win the money within the next hour so that we can get it transferred to John before the banks in the East close."

Kynan nodded and began to inch his way through the crowd of people around the table. When he was in position, he placed his bet.

To Jenna's relief, their plan went off without a hitch. Within forty minutes Kynan accumulated an impressive pile of chips as well as a cheering section from among the other gamblers.

"Way to go!" a young man yelled at Kynan as he won yet again.

Kynan looked around at the encouraging crowd, confused by their reaction. They didn't know him at all and yet they seemed so happy that he was winning.

He glanced over the head of a young woman with an improbable shade of blue hair and caught Jenna's eye. She mouthed the word *Quit*. Only too happy to comply, Kynan scooped up his chips—to the obvious disappointment of the onlookers.

The dealer looked at him in surprise. "You're quitting?"

"I've won enough," Kynan said.

The dealer shrugged. "It takes all kinds," he said as he passed the dice to the next player.

Kynan shouldered his way through the crowd, accepting congratulations from strangers as he went.

"Why are they so pleased I won?" he asked Jenna when he finally reached her.

"Most people wish others well. That's not to say they wouldn't prefer to be the one to win, but they don't begrudge you yours. Now, by my calculations, we have an extra thousand or so more than we need. Come on. Let's get these cashed in."

Jenna hurried toward the cashier's windows to redeem the chips.

"Wow!" The bored look on the teller's face vanished as he saw the pile of chips Kynan pushed toward him. He picked one up and stared at it.

"We won them at the craps table," Jenna offered.

"Hmm." The man looked around as if seeking guidance. It came in the form of a middle-aged man who appeared beside them.

"Congratulations on your win, sir." The man nodded to the teller who promptly began to count the chips. "I've never seen such a run of luck. How'd you do it?" The man gave them a practiced smile that made Jenna nervous.

She surreptitiously stepped on Kynan's foot to warn him not to say anything and then glanced around as if checking to make sure there were no spies in the vicinity. "We have a system," she confided.

"A system?" The man glanced from her to Kynan and then back to her when Kynan remained silent.

Jenna nodded. "Uh-huh. We only gamble when the stars are in the proper alignment, and never for more than a hundred thousand or so."

The man unexpectedly laughed. "Like not overfishing a stream?"

"Something like that," Jenna agreed, feeling guilty at how well he was taking the casino's loss. She and Kynan might need that money, but they didn't really have any moral right to take it. Maybe after Kynan tried to contact his compatriots and failed, he'd resell the diamond and donate the money to Gamblers Anonymous, she thought, to appease her conscience.

"Enjoy your winnings," the man said and melted back into the crowd.

"Your winnings total $104,000 dollars. How do you want it?" the teller asked.

"A cashier's check for $100,000, the rest in cash," Jenna answered.

"And your name, sir?" The man looked at Kynan.

"Kynan."

"And your last name?"

"Phelan."

"And your social security number?" the teller continued.

Kynan shot a quick glance at Jenna.

"Have you forgotten it again? He's absolutely no good with numbers," Jenna improvised.

The teller glanced from the pile of chips to Kynan. "No good with numbers?" he repeated incredulously.

"But he's very lucky," she said. "Fortunately, I know his social security number." She reeled off one that sounded vaguely like hers, praying that the man had no way to check if it was real. To get this close to success and then have it all come undone because she hadn't thought of a basic thing like Kynan having a social security number, was too painful to even contemplate.

To her relief, the clerk merely copied down the number she gave him, and then shoved a piece of paper at Kynan. "Sign on the bottom line," the teller told him. "And don't forget that federal law requires us to report all cash payments of this size to the IRS, so the government'll be wanting their share.''

Jenna's eyes instinctively strayed to the front of Kynan's shirt where the crystal was hidden. That wouldn't be the only thing the feds would want if they found out about this little escapade.

"Their share?" Kynan asked Jenna as the teller moved away to cut the check.

"Taxes," she elaborated. "It's when the government takes part of your salary and redistributes it to various groups with political clout. Didn't you have taxes?"

Kynan shook his head. "Not like that. All companies making a product for sale paid a percentage of their profits to the government. Individuals didn't."

Jenna sighed. "Just my luck. Paradise has already come and gone."

"It wasn't all perfect," Kynan conceded as one particularly acrimonious government dispute surfaced from his memory. "We had our share of pettiness and bickering. It just never escalated to the level that seems to be normal here. We—" He broke off as the teller returned, handed Kynan a check and counted out the rest of his winnings in cash.

"Come on." Jenna urged Kynan toward the bank of public telephones beside the elevators. "We need to call John and tell him that we're wiring him the money. With any luck we should be on the one o'clock flight back to El Paso."

Jenna was idly studying the varied clientele of the casino as she waited in line to use a phone when her attention was suddenly snagged by a man wearing a dark green uniform. She leaned around the pudgy man in front of her to get a better view.

It couldn't be, she tried to convince herself. It just couldn't be.

She forced herself to look again. It was. Unconsciously, she inched closer to Kynan's comforting bulk. Damn! she thought, as anger began to nudge aside her initial fear. Macintosh had no right to hound them like this. They hadn't done anything wrong. At least, nothing more than bilking the casino out of the hundred thousand or so; she squirmed mentally under the lash of her conscience. But nevertheless, it wasn't Macintosh's concern.

"What's the matter?" Kynan asked.

"Don't look now, but I just saw Macintosh. Over by the roulette table."

"You're sure?"

"I'm not likely to forget his face. It's beginning to haunt my dreams. That blasted man is more persistent than the IRS."

Kynan looked confused. "The what?"

"Never mind. The problem is what are we going to do about Macintosh?"

Kynan stared off into space for a long moment and then said, "I think we ought to ignore him. Let's just do what we came to do and see how he responds."

Jenna sighed. "That's probably our best option, but I still don't like it. He must have followed us out to the airport and gotten on the plane after we did."

"Forget Macintosh. It's your turn." Kynan nodded toward a now vacant phone.

Jenna tried to ignore Macintosh, but it was not easy. He followed them to the bank and remained behind one of the large marble columns in the lobby while Jenna arranged to send the funds to John. Then he followed them to the airport and sat two rows away as they waited to board their flight.

To Jenna's relief, Macintosh was seated near the back of the huge plane, while they were directly behind first class.

"I can hardly wait to get home," Jenna said after the stewardess had given them drinks. "I don't think I'm cut out for all this intrigue."

"It will soon be over," Kynan consoled her. "We'll be back home and..."

"And?" Jenna felt a spurt of excitement at the glow that seemed to light his eyes from within.

"You are the most remarkable woman I have ever met in my entire one hundred and eighty-six years," he said softly.

Jenna grinned at him. "Don't tell me I've attracted a member of the geriatric set? Tell me, if I'm thirty-four by the way we calculate years, how old would I be by your calculations? One hundred and seventy-something?"

Kynan frowned at her. "What are you talking about?"

"About how you calculate time."

"A year is measured as the time it takes the Earth to make one complete revolution around the sun," Kynan said. "That hasn't changed in just ten thousand years."

"But... You can't really be a hundred and eighty-six!" she protested. "You'd be dead."

"A fallacy, since I'm not. Are you making a joke?"

Jenna stared at him, her eyes widening as she suddenly remembered something from her Sunday-school days. Weren't those early people in the Bible supposed to have lived for over a thousand years?

"Kynan, how long did people live in Atlantis?"

"On average, about fifteen hundred years."

Jenna gulped. "Fifteen..." She closed her eyes in disbelief. It couldn't be. There had to be some mistake. She didn't care how long it took the sun to go anywhere. People didn't live that long.

"How long do people live now?" Kynan asked, not understanding why she was so upset.

"On average, somewhere into their seventies," Jenna reluctantly told him.

An icy sensation trickled through Kynan's mind, slowing his thought processes. Seventy years? The number reverberated through him like a death knell. That nice old Mrs. Coltrain wasn't old at all, he realized in shock. In his world she would have been considered too young to be given any real responsibility. And Jenna... His Jenna only had another forty years to live. Panic ripped through him. He wanted to grab her and run. But run where? He squelched his fear and forced himself to think rationally instead of emotionally.

Something must have happened when the meteorites hit the Earth. Something had damaged the survivors' immune systems so they could no longer regenerate themselves the way he could. And that mutation had been passed down from generation to generation until today such a pitifully short life-span was thought to be normal.

His Jenna was condemned to die in only forty years. She couldn't die. He wouldn't allow it. But how... The restorative back at the suspension chamber! He suddenly remembered that they had packed far more than he needed to cover any accidents that might occur.

Thoughtfully, he drummed his fingertips on the tray in front of him. From the little he'd read, the only difference between his and Jenna's immune system was that his was fully functional while hers barely functioned. But what if he was wrong and there was another difference? What if giving her the restorative shortened the already minuscule amount of time she had left?

"I really don't mind," Jenna lied. It seemed intolerable to her that she would age and finally die while Kynan would remain exactly the same. He'd continue on with his life and eventually she'd be nothing more than a dim memory of something that had happened long ago.

"I mind." His husky voice comforted her. "Jenna, do you remember when I first woke up, I drank a clear fluid?"

She nodded.

"It's purpose was to reactivate my immune system. There's some left. If we get a book on human physiology and then go out to the chamber, I could run the information through the computer and find out if it's safe for you to take the restorative. If it is, you can drink it and there's a good chance it would repair your immune system and you'd have the life span you were meant to have."

Sure she would, she thought sceptically. Men had been searching for the fountain of youth forever, and they hadn't found it yet. If Kynan's branch of mankind lived fifteen hundred years, it was because their genetic makeup was different; drinking some restorative wasn't going to change that.

Thoughtfully, she studied his worried expression. If her drinking it meant so much to Kynan, it wouldn't hurt to humor him, she finally decided. Besides, if he thought she was going to live as long as he was, he'd continue to treat her as an equal instead of pitying her. Drinking an Atlantean potion was a small price to pay to maintain the status quo.

"I'm game," she said. "When you get your transmitter together again—"

"We'll stop for a book as soon as we get off the plane and then we'll go out to the cave," Kynan said flatly. He'd waited this long to contact his fellow Atlanteans; one more day wouldn't matter.

"Remember our own personal bird dog who's riding in the back of the plane? What are you going to do about him?" she asked dryly.

He'd do whatever was necessary to protect Jenna's future, Kynan thought fiercely. He had never deliberately harmed another living thing in his entire life, but if Macintosh tried to stop him from helping Jenna . . .

"We'll lose him in the mall when we buy the physiology book," he finally said, seeing no reason to worry her.

* * *

Where were they? Macintosh rounded the end of the bookshelf where Farron and Anderson had been standing just minutes before. He glanced up the aisle and then hurried to the next. Both were empty. He rushed out of the bookstore into the mall and was immediately swallowed up by the crowds of late-afternoon shoppers.

Damn! he thought angrily, and then wished he hadn't indulged his rage as his chest began to ache. Deliberately, he tried to relax his muscles. When the pain finally subsided, he made a circuit of the common area outside the bookstore, but didn't find them.

He'd lost them. And it was his own fault. He'd gotten careless because they'd made no attempt to shake him in Vegas or on the way to the mall.

Slowly Macintosh made his way toward the escalator, knowing that climbing the stairs was more than he could handle right now. It had been a long day, and he was dead tired. As well as very confused. He didn't know why they'd flown to Las Vegas. Nor did he know how they'd won all that money. His gut instinct told him that it hadn't been luck. But if not luck then how had they managed to win? he wondered, as he stepped onto the escalator.

He'd watched Anderson play and he hadn't seen him cheat. Not only that, but he was willing to bet that the casino's security had also been watching. If *they* had noticed anything even vaguely suspicious, they never would have paid out.

But if Anderson did have a way to manipulate the dice, then why had he quit when he had? Why not win even more? Why not go to another casino and do it again? Macintosh stepped off the escalator and headed toward the exit.

Could the game have been rigged by the casino itself? There were plenty of rumors about some of the casinos in Las Vegas being connected to the mob. And he didn't know anything about the casino they'd chosen except that it wasn't one of the more prominent ones. Supposing it was mob controlled and Farron was smuggling drugs for them? What better way to pay her off than allow her to win what was owed? Registering the win in Anderson's name would mean that she would not have to pay taxes on it, and there would be no record to tie her to the money.

A sense of excitement gripped him, constricting his breathing. It made beautiful sense. If he could just figure out how to prove it before it was too late.

"Hurry up." Kynan chivied Jenna as she pressed the automatic garage-door opener to lower the door. "I want you to take the restorative, now."

"Just as soon as I get a cold drink." Jenna pushed open the door into the house.

She watched as Kynan yanked open the refrigerator, grabbed a random can of soda and shoved it at her. "Hurry up!" he repeated.

Why was it so important to him that she take it? Jenna wondered. So important that he dragged her directly from the airport to a crowded mall and then out into the desert when she would have expected him to begin immediately to reassemble his transmitter so that it would be ready when the diamond arrived.

Was she more important to him than his dream of contacting the Atlanteans? Jenna found the thought powerfully seductive. Or could it be that deep down he knew there wasn't anyone out there to contact? Maybe she came under the heading of "a bird in the hand"?

Her gaze dropped to Kynan's long fingers as he deftly opened the complicated lid on the vial of restorative. She wouldn't mind being in his hands, she thought dreamily. In fact, it sounded like the perfect ending to a hectic day. She trailed after him into the living room.

"Why is that red light on your telephone flashing?" Kynan asked.

"It means there's a message." Jenna pushed the Play button and the nonthreatening sound of John Warton's voice filled the room telling her that he'd bought the diamond, that the dealer had agreed to cut it tomorrow morning and that he'd send it by special courier either late tomorrow or early the next day.

"Good," Kynan said with satisfaction. "It'll take me that long to reassemble the parts. In the meantime, drink this."

Jenna set down her soda and accepted the container. She looked at Kynan and her gaze was ensnared by the blue sparks dancing in his eyes. An unexpected wave of longing washed over her, catching her by surprise. If only this potion really could work. If only she could have all those years to spend with him. But he hadn't asked her to spend her life with him, she reminded herself soberly.

"If you drink it, I'll give you some Rocky Road ice cream," Kynan offered as a bribe.

"You mean there's some left after the way you've been wolfing it down?"

"I've got a quart secreted in the back of the freezer," he confided. "Behind those disgusting little green things you tried to foist off on me last night."

"Brussels sprouts are good for you," she responded automatically. "They make your hair curly."

"I don't want curly hair. I want you to drink the restorative."

Cautiously, she sniffed the liquid. It didn't smell. Taking a deep breath, she raised the tube and swallowed its contents in one gulp.

She pursed her lips consideringly and stared into the now empty container. It didn't have a taste, either. It had felt warm going down, but not unpleasantly so. She closed her eyes and focused on her body. Nothing felt even slightly out of the ordinary.

"Well?" Kynan demanded.

"Well, what?"

"Did you drink it?"

She handed him the empty vial and took a step toward the couch, only to grab for him when a wave of dizziness swept over her.

Kynan gathered her into his arms and, carrying her to the chair, sat down with her in his lap.

"I almost fell," she said in surprise. "What happened?"

"Momentary disorientation. It'll pass."

"It had better or I'm in deep trouble."

"You worry too much."

Jenna tilted her head back and stared at him in disbelief. "I worry too much!" she repeated incredulously. "I have a man from the past—the far-distant past—hiding out in my house, I've just bilked a casino out of a hundred thousand dollars, I've got the Army following me on a regular basis, and you think I worry too much. God forbid that I should ever find out what you consider worthy of a little worrying."

"My poor darling." Kynan gently massaged the tense muscles at the base of her neck. "Once I manage to make contact with the Atlanteans, all your troubles will be over."

Her troubles would be over a lot sooner if Kynan would just make contact with reality, Jenna thought ruefully. But then dreams die hard for everyone. She shivered at the slightly roughened texture of his fingers as they scraped enticingly across her skin. His hand felt warm. Warm and disconcerting. Even more disconcerting was the feel of his hardening masculinity beneath her hips.

Jenna snuggled her face against his neck and breathed deeply of the scent that clung to his skin. It was a heady mixture of soap, sunlight and desert plants. Underlying all that was the less easily categorized smell of the man himself. She pressed closer. Her action pushed her breasts into his chest, and she felt a tingling sensation skitter along her nerve endings.

Jenna focused on the tantalizing feeling, trying to define it. To label it so that she could understand exactly why Kynan's kisses were so different. It wasn't as if she'd never been kissed before—because she had—but none of them had done more than cause a slight ripple on the surface of her emotions. Why hadn't she experienced even a tiny fraction of what she felt when Kynan touched her?

Jenna linked her arms around Kynan's neck and, tilting her head to one side, studied him, wondering what he'd look like when he was finally old. She squinted slightly, trying to imagine him with white hair and wrinkles, but her eyes didn't seem to be working right.

"What's the matter?" he asked.

"You're fuzzy."

He chuckled. "Is that an indictment of my thinking?"

"More likely an indictment of your restorative. Not only that, but..."

She watched as a shimmering halo of light seemed to vibrate around his head. Tiny flecks of color, ranging from brilliant yellow to a regal purple, randomly winked in and out of existence. She smiled dreamily. Even though logic told her that what she was seeing was undoubtedly the result of his drink's potency, it didn't distract from its beauty.

"You're a creature of the light and all its prismatic parts," she announced pensively. "I particularly like that reddish-orange spark right there." She tried to capture it with her mouth. She missed, her lips landing against his chin. So she consoled herself by tasting his skin with the tip of her tongue.

"Jenna?" Kynan grasped her narrow shoulders and held her back from him as he stared down into her face. "What are you talking about?"

"That orangish spark of color," she said. "You look as if someone ground up a rainbow for confetti and tossed a handful of it all over you. I like it," she assured him.

Kynan frowned. "I'm not sure I do. The machine said that it might interfere with your cognitive powers for a few hours, but it didn't say anything about your seeing things."

"Interfere with my cognitive... You mean as in 'drunk'?" she asked curiously.

"No, I mean as in 'interfere with your cognitive powers.'"

"Half a dozen of one, six of another. But your precious computer is wrong. My thinking is just fine. It's my vision that's having trouble. But you know I rather like it." She giggled, feeling incredibly lighthearted and very much in control of the situation. "It's kind of like having built-in rose-colored glasses."

"You'll feel more yourself shortly."

"And how do you feel?" she asked solemnly. "Let me see...."

She ran her fingertips along his cheek. "You feel warm and smooth and..." She traced around the edges of his ear. "Cartilage feels different. Hard and unyielding. Overall, I think I prefer the skin on your cheeks."

"Perhaps you should lie down," Kynan said worriedly.

She nodded decisively. "Excellent idea. Would you help me over to the couch?"

"Certainly." Kynan carried her to the couch and set her down on it. When he went to move away, Jenna grabbed hold of his shirt and yanked.

"Sit down." She patted the couch beside her hips. "I haven't finished yet."

He obligingly sat down. "Finished what?"

"Exploring how you feel." She tugged his shirt out of his pants and slowly ran her palms up over his chest. His skin was hotter there.

"And how do I feel?" Kynan's voice deepened and his obvious reaction to her touch heightened Jenna's growing sense of excitement.

"You feel..." She flicked her fingernail over his flat masculine nipple and a satisfied smile curved her lips at his sudden jerk.

"I need more input," she said and began to unbutton his shirt. Her fingers were clumsy, and it was hard to make them do what she wanted. Finally she managed to worry his last button free, and she shoved the shirt back over his shoulders. It fell unheeded to the floor.

"Now then, let me see." She leaned against the back of the couch and studied the tantalizing expanse of his chest intently. Where to start? With the enticing pulse at the base of his throat? She placed a kiss in the center of it and watched, fascinated, as his pulse rate increased frantically.

Jenna peered at Kynan through slitted eyes. The laugh lines around his mouth were more deeply indented, but he didn't look as if he found this funny. In fact, when Jenna stared into his blazing green eyes, he looked as if he were firmly caught in the throes of something he couldn't entirely control. She felt a surge of triumph. She had caused that reaction. She, unsophisticated Jenna Farron, had the power to drive a gorgeous hunk like Kynan to the edge of distraction. She smiled secretively. Now all she had to do was push him over the edge.

She scooted closer to him. "Of course, there are many ways to touch besides just with the hands."

Kynan nodded gravely. "The entire surface of the skin is a sense organ. And that being the case..." To her surprise, he suddenly stood and, unzipping his jeans, shoved them and his briefs down over his legs and kicked them aside.

Jenna swallowed and slowly licked her tongue over her suddenly dry lips. Kynan was so quintessentially masculine. He was everything she had ever fantasized about, and he was all hers.

"We need to widen this research of yours." Kynan pulled her shirt over her head and tossed it aside. Reverently, he rushed the backs of his knuckles over her silk-covered breasts. Jenna could feel her sensitive flesh contracting with desire, and she wanted more. Much more.

Reaching behind her, she unfastened her bra. She wanted to feel Kynan's weight pressing against her. Wanted it with a fervor that bordered on obsession. Grasping his shoulders, she pulled him down to her.

Reaction poured over her in waves at the feel of his body hair abrading the hypersensitive tips of her breasts. She ran her hands down over his powerful arms, rubbing and squeezing the muscles as she went. A heavy, dragging sensation oozed through her, turning her bones to a semisolid that wanted to reform themselves to fit his every contour.

Jenna sighed in pure delight as Kynan began to nibble the pliant flesh of her neck, and she arched her head back to allow him better access.

Kynan's lips moved up over her chin to find her mouth and he nibbled enticingly on her lower lip. Jenna threaded her fingers through his silky hair to hold him still so she could deepen the kiss. Her mouth opened and his tongue surged inside to engage hers in a duel of sensuality that left her breathless and trembling. Her hands clutched at his shoulders as she tried to pull him closer.

To her dismay, Kynan locked his forearms and resisted her pressure. Instead, he fumbled for the zipper on her shorts.

Jenna dug her heels into the sofa and levered her lower body up so that he could pull her shorts and panties down over her slim hips. Impatiently, she kicked them off her legs and toward the end of the couch.

For a long moment, Kynan simply stared at her. The brilliant glow in his eyes and the desire-hardened planes of his face made her feel omnipotent.

Kynan slowly lowered his body over hers and his heavy weight pressed her down into the sofa. Blind need poured through her, engulfing her. She wiggled beneath him, gasping as the heated length of his manhood brushed against her belly.

"Kynan!" she gasped. "You feel good all over. Everywhere."

His deep chuckle reverberated through her, making her stomach twist with longing. "But Jenna, I haven't been everywhere yet." His hand slipped between her legs, and he gently rubbed his finger over the small center of her desire.

Jenna jerked in reaction as jagged shards of sensation tore through her. She felt as if she'd die if he stopped now.

"Kynan, I..." she managed to force out past her clenched teeth. "I..."

"What, my precious one?" His warm breath drifted over her face at the same time his finger slipped inside her, exploring her moistness.

"Kynan," she gritted out, "quit playing."

"But I'm not playing. I've never been more serious about anything in my life."

His words echoed meaninglessly through Jenna's disoriented mind. She was totally wrapped up in her own needs. Needs that absolutely had to be assuaged before she burst into flames.

As if Kynan understood and shared her sense of urgency, he positioned himself and then pushed forward, filling her with one sure stroke.

Sensation upon exquisite sensation ripped through her, and Jenna felt as if her whole being were tightening around him. Eddying waves of reaction spiraled through her, making her frantic.

Just when she thought she couldn't stand any more, her body convulsed in release, sending her hurtling into a rainbow-lit world of pure sensation. Glittering lines of silvery light whirled through her and around her until she wanted to weep from the beauty of it.

Dimly she was aware of Kynan's muffled shout as he
ound his own satisfaction, but only dimly. At that mo-
ient, nothing had any reality for her but her own feelings.
Gradually the wonder began to fade, and she slowly drifted
ack to full awareness to find Kynan's limp body sprawled
ver her. She snuggled her face against his damp shoulder,
rying to hang on to the feeling of euphoria she'd been rid-
ng.

But the real world and all its attendant problems preyed
n her mind. Particularly, what to do about Kynan and his
uture. She nibbled worriedly on her lower lip.

She couldn't keep Kynan as a kind of pensioner. At the
noment he was content to pour all his considerable energy
nd intelligence into contacting survivors of Atlantis, but
ooner or later he'd have to admit that there weren't any.
And he'd turn to other things. But *what* other things? What
ould he do in this world in which he'd so unexpectedly
ound himself?

She remembered the teller at the casino who'd wanted
Kynan's social security number. Kynan not only didn't have
ne, he didn't have any of the identification men his age
ormally had.

She knew from reading the local papers that fake identi-
ies could be bought rather easily along the border. But she
ery much doubted that those kinds of forged documents
vould stand up to much scrutiny. They would only work if
Kynan was content to keep out of sight.

She tilted her head back and stared up at him, relieved to
ee that the effects of the restorative had disappeared. The
parkling lights were gone. Kynan's eyes were closed, and
here was a slight smile lifting the corners of his mouth.
Even in repose, the strong determined lines of his face
lominated. No. Kynan would never be content to hide away.
He'd undoubtedly invent something or patent one of those

machines from his era and suddenly find himself in the spotlight.

What was the answer? The question nagged at her. How did one establish an identity for a grown man that would withstand an investigation? She didn't know. All she knew was that she had to do it. Because by protecting Kynan's future, she was also ensuring her own.

Eight

'It's finally done," Kynan announced tiredly.

Jenna studied the reconstructed transmitter that had consumed virtually all of Kynan's time as well as his thoughts for the past two days. It was not an impressive-looking sight, and didn't look capable of getting a message to the next town, never mind the next star system.

"What do we do now?" she asked.

"We activate it." Kynan reached toward the transmitter.

"No!" Jenna yelped and grabbed his arm. "When we tried out the first transmitter it was only on for a few seconds, but this will probably be on long enough to give Macintosh a good shot at tracing it. Right to my living room."

"I'm using a different type of signal in this transmitter. Your technology isn't advanced enough to pick it up."

"You don't know that for a fact," Jenna insisted. "The government has lots of inventions that are not public knowledge."

Kynan stared down at the transmitter, a considering expression on his face. "You could be right. How about if we activate it in an isolated area?"

"Not the cave. I don't want to risk that."

"No, not the cave," Kynan agreed. "Somewhere a few miles from it. We'll set up the transmitter in the desert, and we can monitor an answer on that." He gestured toward a small black box about the size of a pack of cigarettes on the coffee table.

"You don't like the idea?" he asked, at her worried expression.

"It's not that.... The problem is how do we get past Macintosh to set up the transmitter in the first place? He's practically camped outside the house since we got back from Las Vegas."

Jenna cautiously cracked the door and peered down the street, squinting in the bright morning sunlight. Fear, exasperation and anger churned through her at the sight of Macintosh's car.

"Blast that man, anyway," she muttered. "Why won't he go away? Or do something?"

"I imagine he's waiting for us to do something."

Jenna glanced back at the transmitter. "And that thing might well be it. For all I know there's some kind of federal law against signaling other star systems without a license!"

"We need to get rid of him long enough to get the transmitter in place and functioning," Kynan said slowly. "Do you have any ideas?"

"None that are legal. Or moral. He's getting harder to shake."

"We could wait until he leaves. He has to go home sometime."

"Yeah, but last night he didn't go till almost ten. And wandering around in the desert at night is asking for trouble. I wonder which of us he'd follow if he thought we weren't together?"

"What?"

"We don't really know which of us he's most interested in," Jenna explained. "I assumed it was you because I know where you came from. But supposing I'm the one he suspects of whatever it is he suspects?"

Kynan nodded. "Which leads to your question of which would he follow. But how's that going to help us? I can't drive the truck, and you can't activate the machine."

"True, but suppose you were to crouch down on the floorboards of the truck before I drive out of the garage. From where Macintosh is parked, it'll look like I'm by myself. He might think I'm just heading out into the desert to look for artifacts as I've been doing all summer, so he might stay behind to see what you get up to."

"It's worth a try," Kynan decided.

"And if he does follow me, I'll simply stop at a convenience store, buy something, then circle around and come back. Then we can come up with another plan."

Kynan picked up the small box and handed it to her. "Here, you carry this, and I'll bring the transmitter." He squatted down and picked it up.

Appreciatively, Jenna watched the muscles in Kynan's arms ripple beneath the effort he was making. A flutter of excitement curled through her as she remembered the strength in his arms as he'd bound her pliant body to his. As he'd held her close and kissed her. As he'd—

"Get the door to the garage, will you? And check to see if the anti-gravity device is still in the truck." Kynan's prosaic request interrupted her delightful memories.

Ah, well, Jenna thought as she hurried out to the kitchen, maybe once he satisfied his compulsion to try to reach his compatriots, he'd be willing to put his mind to other things, such as making love to her again. And figuring out how they were going to set him up with an identity so he could move freely in society.

Kynan carefully set his transmitter in the bed of the truck and covered it with the dusty tarp while Jenna fished her sunglasses out of her equipment bag and climbed into the driver's seat. She watched as Kynan attempted to squeeze himself under the dashboard.

"It isn't funny." He took exception to her giggles.

Jenna grinned happily at him, feeling incredibly light-hearted. A feeling she was at a total loss to explain. It certainly wasn't logical. She was involved in all sorts of questionable activities that skirted the law. She should be nervous and scared. But she wasn't.

The truth was, Kynan made her feel happy. Complete. He gave her a whole new perspective on life, and she liked it. She liked it very much. So much so, that she was willing to face down any number of Colonel Macintoshes in order to hang on to that feeling. And to Kynan.

To her surprise, Kynan took hold of her red cotton T-shirt and tugged her toward him. The heat from his body washed over her, sending prickles of awareness dancing along her nerve endings. Intrigued, Jenna stared into his eyes. They were sparkling with what she suspected was pure devilment.

Fascinated, she stared at them. Kynan had such beautiful eyes. Huge rings of exquisite color that promised so much. Longingly her gaze dropped to his lips and a craving to feel them pressed against her own swept through her.

It was a wish that Kynan obviously shared. His fingers curled around the nape of her neck, and he pulled her closer.

With a sigh, Jenna relaxed against him, meeting his lips. They were warm and firm and tasted faintly of chocolate. She shivered as his mouth opened and the tip of his tongue traced over her closed lips. A surge of desire slammed through her, and she moved restlessly beneath the onslaught of sensation, wincing when her head made contact with one of the knobs on the dashboard. She raised her head and peered down into Kynan's face. His eyes were still closed and his lips were lifted in a sensual curl that made her want to drag him back into the house and make mad, passionate love to him.

She firmly squelched the provocative thought and, scrambling upright, buckled her seat belt. They had things to do, she told herself. And indulging her libido wasn't one of them. If they were going to outwit Macintosh, she had to keep her wits about her.

She lifted her right hand and muttered, "We who are about to die, salute you."

"What!"

"It's from Latin. Keep your head down," she ordered as she pressed the button on the automatic garage-door opener.

Macintosh hastily tossed his book onto the seat beside him as Farron's truck pulled out into the street. He squinted in the sunlight, trying to get a better view through her vehicle's tinted windows, then glanced back at the house when he realized she was alone. Since Anderson hadn't already left, he must still be there. Macintosh frowned in indecision as her truck slowly moved down the street. Farron didn't seem to be in any hurry. He watched as she waved to the old lady who seemed to spend an inordinate amount of time in her front yard tending her flowers.

According to what he'd been able to find out, Farron normally spent her days in the desert, supposedly searching for artifacts. She hadn't gone anywhere in several days. Maybe she was simply reverting to form. He watched as she came to a stop at the corner and waited for the traffic to clear.

Thoughtfully he turned back to the house. Was she a decoy to lure him away so Anderson could meet with their contact in the drug cartel? Should he follow her or should he wait and see who came calling on Anderson?

Damn! he thought in frustration. If only Washington would get in gear and respond to his query on Anderson's fingerprints. It was intolerable that he should have to wait this long to hear anything.

He'd stay here, he finally decided as Jenna pulled onto the main road. Anderson was probably his best bet. Farron was undoubtedly heading into the desert to maintain the fiction that her sole interest was archaeology.

Macintosh leaned back against the headrest and waited.

Some time later the sound of his cellular phone caught him by surprise. He turned the radio down and grabbed it.

"Macintosh, here."

"You asked me to call you when you received a reply from that query you sent off to Washington, sir." Macintosh recognized the voice of the clerk who worked for Major Defton.

"Well, a thick manila envelope just arrived by special messenger for you, Colonel."

Macintosh glanced over at Farron's house. There had been no movement of any kind since she'd left. Maybe he was wrong. Maybe Anderson didn't have a meeting set up.

"Colonel, are you there?"

"Yes. Listen, is Captain Bradshaw in his office?"

"Yes, sir."

"Have him bring the package out to Farron's house."

"He can't, Sir. It's marked secret, to be released only on your signature."

Macintosh studied Farron's house speculatively. "Ask Captain Bradshaw to meet me here at Farron's. If he can't get away, call me back."

"Yes, sir. I will." The line went dead, and Macintosh switched it off. He might be wasting Artie's time, but if there was a meeting set up, he couldn't afford to miss it. There was so little time left. A momentary spurt of panic escalated the ever-present pain in his chest. In five short days he went in for his checkup, and if he hadn't cracked this case by then, he could forget his future. Forget everything that mattered to him. Everything he'd worked so hard to attain.

It would be okay, he told himself, closing his eyes and trying to relax while he waited for Artie.

It was almost an hour later before Macintosh was able to get back to the office. As the clerk had said, the manila envelope was thick. He picked it up with fingers that trembled in eagerness. Ripping it open, he shook the contents onto his desk. Papers and pictures drifted down.

He quickly riffled through them, extracting a letter. Eagerly, he read it. According to his contact in the FBI, there was no record anywhere of Anderson's fingerprints: not on an arrest record, not in the military, not on any application form of any kind, not on a passport application, not on a job application and not on any state's driver's license.

He glanced at the top of the letter and caught the heading which proclaimed it to be one of two. Hurriedly, he found the second page. His contact went on to say that he had obtained pictures of every visiting professor at Farron's university and Macintosh should check to make sure that the man in question wasn't one of them. He concluded by saying that he had asked a Swedish operative to run Kynan's prints through their files and they, too, had no record of him.

Macintosh carefully examined each picture. None of them was even vaguely familiar. Which meant he'd been right, he thought in satisfaction. From wherever it was Anderson had sprung, it wasn't the United States. Nor, apparently, Sweden. Chances were very good he was in the States illegally.

That possibility might be enough to involve the border patrol, Macintosh decided. Especially if he talked fast and kept stressing national security.

He could ask to have a border-patrol agent go with him to Farron's house and have the agent demand to see proof that Anderson had a legal right to be in this country. And if, as he suspected, Anderson couldn't produce proof, it would give him the excuse he needed to get a search warrant issued for Farron's house. If he could just search the place, surely he'd find something to tie the pair to drug smuggling. All he needed was one solid fact and he could arrest the two of them and get credit for cracking the ring before he turned the case over to the FBI.

He reached for the phone. With any luck at all, he'd have this whole thing tied up in time to make the six o'clock news.

"Now all we have to do is wait," Kynan said.

And wait and wait, Jenna mentally added. She stole a quick glance at Kynan as she turned off the main road into her subdivision. Tension had etched deep lines across his face, and she could see the tightly clenched muscles of his jaw beneath his skin. Her gaze dropped to the small black box he was clutching like a lifeline. He was clearly nervous, but was it because he thought rescue was at hand or because deep down he knew better?

"How long do you think it will be before you hear anything?" she asked cautiously.

"I don't know. A day, two at the most."

A day or two? Jenna felt a hysterical urge to laugh. The U.S. Postal Service couldn't get a letter from New York to Philadelphia in two days and he expected to hear from God-only-knew-where in the same amount of time?

"There's Mrs. Coltrain." Kynan returned the old woman's wave. "I think she wants us to stop."

Jenna obligingly pulled up in front of Mrs. Coltrain's house and cut the engine.

"Good afternoon, Mrs. Coltrain," Jenna gave her a warm smile. "How does your garden grow?"

Mrs. Coltrain nodded conspiratorially. "Never you mind my garden. It's my suspicions that are growing."

"Oh?" Jenna resisted the impulse to look at Kynan. "About what?"

"Come into the house, and I'll tell you over coffee." She turned and headed toward the door.

Jenna looked first at Kynan, but he just shook his head as if disclaiming all responsibility for Mrs. Coltrain's suspicions, so Jenna glanced down the street toward the vacant lot. The government car was still parked there. She stifled a sigh. The number of people who were suspicious seemed to be growing by leaps and bounds. Next thing she knew, they'd have the press out here and then the fat would really be in the fire.

"Have you noticed that white car just down the road a ways?" Mrs. Coltrain asked, the minute she'd handed them their coffee.

"It's hard to miss," Jenna said dryly. "Especially since it hasn't moved since sometime early this morning."

Mrs. Coltrain shook her head. "But it has. That's not the same car that was there this morning. That one drove away a couple of hours after you did."

"Oh?" Jenna murmured encouragingly.

"Yes, I was working in my garden when I heard a phone ring. At first I thought it was mine and was about to answer it when I realized it was coming from that white car. He had one of those newfangled car phones."

"And then what happened?" Jenna asked. "He left?"

"Not right away. About half an hour after he got the call, another one of those cars pulled up behind him—government cars is what they are. Anyway, the man inside the second car got out and talked to the first man and then the first man drove away and the second one stayed." Mrs. Coltrain nodded decisively. "I don't like this."

And that is the understatement of the year, Jenna thought grimly. But where did Macintosh go? Had he somehow realized that Kynan wasn't in the house and left to try to find them? But if Macintosh had figured out that they were already gone, then why wait until a replacement came before he left? She had no idea, and her lack of knowledge made her nervous. Very nervous.

"Do you know why the government would be watching our neighborhood?" Mrs. Coltrain asked.

"No," Jenna lied. "Oh, there's Eleanor." Jenna awkwardly changed the subject as the cat wandered into the room.

"Good afternoon, cat." Kynan gravely greeted the feline and was given a hiss of outrage for his trouble.

"Eleanor's a one-person cat," Mrs. Coltrain said, excusing the cat's manners. "Always has been. Why, I remember when I first got her..." She launched into a reminiscence that rolled soothingly over Jenna's taut nerves.

Please, just a few more days, Jenna prayed. If Macintosh would just leave them alone long enough for Kynan to face the fact that he wasn't going to get an answer to his message, then perhaps she could convince him to go back to the university with her. Once they were there, away from the distraction of Macintosh and his suspicions, she could figure out how to fit Kynan into her world.

A few minutes later, Jenna was jerked out of her jumbled thoughts when the cat gave an angry howl and headed toward the front door.

Mrs. Coltrain broke off her story and peered over the top of her bifocals at the animal. "Eleanor probably heard the neighbor's cat," she confided, getting up to let her out. "She's so territorial."

"Maybe we could sic Eleanor on Macintosh," Jenna whispered to Kynan, who was happily devouring the plate of chocolate-chip cookies Mrs. Coltrain had put out.

She turned as Mrs. Coltrain suddenly reappeared, looking flustered. "He's back, and he's got someone else with him."

"He?" Jenna asked.

"That government man who left. He just pulled up behind the car that replaced his and there's a Border Patrol car with him."

Jenna closed her eyes and tried to think, but the icy feeling of blind panic that gripped her made it impossible. Her instinct was to grab hold of Kynan and run. But tempting as the prospect was, she knew it wouldn't work. She had no idea how to go about disappearing. All they'd accomplish by running would be to admit guilt.

Her hand instinctively reached for Kynan, and his hard fingers closed around hers with comforting strength. The warmth of his skin seeped into her chilled flesh, making her feel fractionally better.

"Let's go see what they're doing out there." Kynan pulled Jenna to her feet and went to the front window, trailed by the curious Mrs. Coltrain.

Macintosh didn't notice the curtains fluttering in Mrs. Coltrain's window as he waited impatiently for the Border Patrol agent to get out of his car.

"There." Macintosh pointed to Jenna's truck when the agent joined him. "That's hers. I wonder what's under that tarp in the back?"

"You can wonder all you want," the Border Patrol agent said. "But without a search warrant that's all you'd better do."

Macintosh stared in frustration at the interesting lumps and bumps visible beneath the tarp. "It's parked on a public street."

"The truck is private property," the agent repeated doggedly. "I'm not breaking the law for you. If this guy's an alien, then you can get a search warrant and look, but if you go anywhere near it without a warrant, I'm leaving."

Macintosh audibly ground his teeth. It had taken him the better part of an hour to convince this guy's superior to even have him talk to Anderson. The blind fool thought that Anderson was probably nothing more than somebody's husband who was lying about his identity so that he could carry on a summer affair with Farron without his wife finding out. And he hadn't dared tell the Border Patrol about Farron's connection to Lessing or Lessing's connection to the Colombian drug cartel because if he did, the Border Patrol would immediately turn the whole thing over to the FBI. And the FBI would undoubtedly freeze him out, and he absolutely had to get credit for breaking the ring or he could kiss his Army career goodbye.

"Hey, don't blame me." The agent held out his hands in a disclaiming gesture. "I didn't make the rules. The Constitution did. You got a problem with that, take it up with the Founding Fathers."

If he didn't solve this case quickly, he was liable to do exactly that, Macintosh thought as the pain in his chest increased. In person.

"Look, Colonel, can we get this over with?" the agent demanded. "I have some paperwork to do back at the office before I can go home tonight."

"Let me check with Artie first and see when Farron came back." Macintosh gestured for Artie to join them.

Artie got out of the car and met him halfway.

"Is Farron inside her house?" Macintosh asked.

Artie shook his head. "No. They came back about fifteen minutes ago, and the old lady took them inside her house."

"They?" Macintosh questioned. "She was by herself when she left."

Artie shrugged. "If you say so, but she had the blond guy with her when she returned."

"Blond!" the agent repeated incredulously. "Your illegal alien is a blond?"

"Not all illegals come from Mexico," Macintosh said tightly.

"Down here they do," the agent muttered. "You'd better know what you're doing."

Macintosh ignored him. "Wait here by Farron's truck. We won't be long," he told Artie and then started toward Mrs. Coltrain's house with the agent lagging behind.

"Why, they're coming here." Mrs. Coltrain watched them cross the street.

"Get away from the window," Kynan ordered.

Jenna did. She scurried back to the living room and flopped down on the sofa, breathing a sigh of relief when Kynan sank down beside her. Logically she knew that he was far less able to cope with the authorities than she was, but somehow she felt better when he was beside her.

Mrs. Coltrain hovered in the middle of the living room, an anxious expression on her elderly face.

The sound of the doorbell echoed harshly through the small house. The noise seemed to beat inside Jenna's head like a death knell and unconsciously she inched closer to Kynan.

"I'd better let them in," Mrs. Coltrain said. "If they're anything like the ones in the movies, they'll break my door down."

"Kynan..." Jenna turned to him as Mrs. Coltrain hurried to the door. "I..." Her voice trailed away into nothingness. She didn't know what she wanted to say. She only knew how she felt. Scared to death that she was about to lose him just when she'd found him. But not without a fight. She pressed her lips together. There were still laws.

"Why, look who's come to call." Mrs. Coltrain ushered Macintosh and a strange man wearing the uniform of the Border Patrol back into the living room. "The colonel says he's looking for you, Jenna."

"Actually it's him I'm looking for." Macintosh nodded toward Kynan.

"Well, you've found me." Kynan's soft voice sent a prickle of apprehension down Jenna's spine. She'd been so busy worrying about what she was going to do, she hadn't thought about what Kynan might do. Her fingers tightened on Kynan's wrist, and she sent him a warning glance. They had to outwit Macintosh, not overpower him.

"I presume you have a reason for invading my privacy as well as for your continued harassment of Dr. Farron and myself." Kynan's voice hardened.

Very good, Jenna mentally approved his words. Put Macintosh on the defensive.

"Not me, mister. I'm only here because he—" the agent gestured toward Macintosh "—convinced my superior that you aren't all you should be."

"Not all he should be?" Mrs. Coltrain repeated. "How much more should he be? Why, in my day, we'd have said he was the cat's pajamas."

Jenna giggled as Kynan dropped his gaze to the cat in confusion. Macintosh was not amused.

"I want to see some proof of just who you are," Macintosh demanded.

"On what grounds?" Jenna countered. "You have no right to stop a person on the street and harass them without just cause."

"Colonel?" the agent prompted nervously.

"You told me he was a visiting professor from Sweden, yet his fingerprints aren't on file with any government agency in this country or in Sweden," Macintosh explained triumphantly.

Yeah, how would I explain that? Jenna wondered nervously. Before she could think of a plausible lie, Mrs. Coltrain spoke up unexpectedly.

"Kynan, you naughty boy, I told you not to lie to her."

Kynan, with a quickness Jenna could only applaud, picked up on the cue and hung his head.

"I told him and told him that if you couldn't like him for himself, then you didn't deserve a fine man like him, Jenna," Mrs. Coltrain said. "But he was worried about you being a professor and all and he did like you so very much. So he lied."

"Lied?" Macintosh glanced in confusion from Mrs. Coltrain to the top of Kynan's gleaming blond head, which was all that was visible.

"The young are so foolish," Mrs. Coltrain lamented, and Jenna bit her lip to keep from giggling hysterically. Did Mrs. Coltrain but know it, Kynan was more than twice her age.

"They are so eager to impress and it never works." Mrs. Coltrain gave Kynan a commiserating look. "You see, Kynan is not really a professor. In fact, he doesn't even have a college degree. He wouldn't listen to me and his mother and stay in school. No, he had to quit and—"

"He told her he was a professor from Sweden," Macintosh insisted.

"He's never been to Sweden in his entire life, and I ought to know because he's my grandson," Mrs. Coltrain said. "In fact, I don't think he's been any farther east than Dallas."

"But—" Macintosh began.

"Sweden's so far away, don't you see," Mrs. Coltrain said. "Kynan thought Jenna wouldn't know anything about Sweden. Now, Kynan—" Mrs. Coltrain turned to him "—tell Jenna that you're sorry about lying to her. That was very wrong of you."

Jenna glanced up at Jenna, his green eyes glowing with pure mischief, and muttered, "Sorry."

"S'okay," she muttered back.

The Border Patrol agent grinned sympathetically at Kynan. "I tell you, man, your grandma's right. It's never a good idea to lie to a woman. They always find out in the end and make you pay."

Macintosh shot the agent a fulminating glare, and the man subsided into silence. "You're lying," Macintosh accused.

"But he did tell me that he was from Sweden," Jenna said innocently. "And I believed him."

"If Mrs. Coltrain is willing to swear that this man is her grandson . . ." the Border Patrol agent began.

"I not only say it, I can prove it. Just a moment." Mrs. Coltrain hurried from the room. She was back within minutes waving a piece of yellow paper. "See." She showed it to the Border Patrol agent. "It's Kynan's birth certificate."

Macintosh grabbed the certificate and studied it. "How come this says his name is John David Polanski, and you call him Kynan Anderson?" he demanded.

"Because my poor daughter named him after his father and the man ran away with another woman when Kynan was just a few weeks old. She couldn't bear to hear the name John so we started calling him Kynan." Mrs. Coltrain frowned as if trying to remember. "I think it was from a book she'd read.

"As for Anderson, Kynan made that up because he didn't think Jenna would believe that someone named Polanski was Swedish."

"Thank you, ma'am. I'm sorry to have bothered you." The agent decided enough was enough. "Thank you very much for your cooperation."

"Oh, I don't mind." Mrs. Coltrain smiled gently at him. "I don't get many visitors anymore. Most everybody I know is already dead."

Left with no alternative, Macintosh shoved the birth certificate at her and stomped out after the agent.

"I don't believe her," Macintosh insisted as they crossed the street toward Artie, who was leaning against Jenna's truck.

"It doesn't matter what you believe," the agent said. "The law has rules, and we follow them. If you can prove that the old woman is lying, although I don't know why she would, then we'll look into it again. Until then, the Border Patrol is satisfied that the guy's a citizen with a right to be here. Good afternoon." He nodded to the two men and, climbing into his car, drove away.

Macintosh watched him go with a feeling of intense frus-
ration that was mirrored in his aching chest.

"No luck?" Artie asked.

"No, they had a glib little story prepared that that idiot
swallowed."

Artie shrugged. "Maybe, but the guy didn't strike me as
stupid. Mac..." He paused as if trying to figure out how to
phrase his comment. "Has it occurred to you that you're
getting to be just the least bit obsessive about the pair of
them? Maybe it really is nothing more than a coincidence
that Lessing was willing to allow Farron on his land or that
Anderson suddenly appeared immediately after the radar
interference.

"Sure," Macintosh scoffed. "And maybe Winkler was
right after all and everything was caused by little green men
from Mars. I tell you, Artie, they're lying. I can smell it. I
just have to prove it."

He reached into his pocket and pulled out a small silver
disk about two inches in diameter. He glanced toward Mrs.
Coltrain's house to make sure that they couldn't see him and
then stuck the disk beneath the rear fender of Jenna's truck.

"What was that?" Artie asked.

"A tracking device," Macintosh said in satisfaction.
"Now let them try and lose me."

Artie simply shook his head. "You're making a mistake,
Mac. The way you're going you're liable to wind up with a
harassment charge filed against you."

Or dead. Macintosh resisted the impulse to press his fist
against his chest in an attempt to ease the escalating pain.
His disappointment was almost tangible. He'd so counted
on being able to wrap this up tonight and now... A sense of
discouragement filled him.

When Macintosh didn't respond to his warning, Artie
shrugged and started toward his car. "I hope you know what
you're doing," he said.

I'm fighting for my life, Macintosh thought grimly as he watched Artie drive away. And right now the odds didn't look too good. Despite the danger of openly tangling with a drug cartel on his own, he was going to have to push Farron and Anderson harder and hope they made a mistake he could use against them.

He climbed into his car and started it up. With the tracking device in place, he no longer had to maintain visual contact. He only needed to stay within a mile of them. He decided to park on the street behind this one and wait to see what developed.

"He's leaving," Jenna announced from her spot behind Mrs. Coltrain's front window curtain. "I wonder if he's given up."

"I doubt it." Kynan pressed closer so that he could see, too. Jenna swallowed uneasily at the feel of his heavily muscled body pressing against her from shoulder to hip. It was a heady sensation. But this wasn't the time to be indulging her senses. She determinedly stepped back.

"Mrs. Coltrain," Jenna said, "thank you very much for your help. Kynan hasn't really done anything wrong."

Mrs. Coltrain smiled at her. "I know that, Jenna. Kynan is a dear, sweet boy. I wish he really were my grandson."

"I would be proud to have you for a grandmother," Kynan said gently.

"Macintosh will know you aren't when he checks the records," Jenna suddenly realized.

"No, he won't." Mrs. Coltrain looked sad.

"Why not?" Jenna asked her.

"Because I'm the only one who knows what happened to my grandson. And since John never was in the army or anything like that, there are no records of his fingerprints anywhere."

Jenna felt a surge of excitement. This could well be the answer to the problem of how to provide Kynan with an identity that would pass official scrutiny. If only the real grandson didn't suddenly reappear.

Mrs. Coltrain stared blindly off into space as if looking down a long corridor of time. "It all seems so long ago," she murmured. "Almost like it happened to another person. You see, my daughter's husband really did desert her when John was only a tiny baby. So they came to live with me. I was a widow and I was glad to have them, but..."

She shook her head unhappily. "John was never... quite normal. He seemed to like hurting things. When I tried to talk to the doctor about it, the man just kept saying it was a phrase and John would outgrow it. Then he got to be a teenager, and he was totally beyond our control. His mother cried and I prayed and neither approach worked. He finally ran away to California.

"It might seem like a terrible thing to say about your own flesh and blood, but I was glad when he left. It was peaceful without him. At least it was until a couple of years later when my daughter was diagnosed with breast cancer. She wanted so badly to see John again. The only thing that was keeping her alive toward the end was her compulsion to see him just once more before she died."

"You don't have to tell me this," Jenna said, worried about how the unhappy memories would affect Mrs. Coltrain.

"No." Mrs. Coltrain shook her head. "I want you to understand why Kynan can be John if he wants. A few months before my daughter died, she was in the hospital when I got a call from the police in Los Angeles. They said that a man had been killed during a robbery at a liquor store and from the identification he had on him they thought it was my grandson and would I come and identify the body."

Mrs. Coltrain shuddered, and Kynan gripped her shoulder comfortingly. She smiled sadly at him and continued. "I didn't say anything to my daughter because I was afraid of how she'd take it. So I flew out, and it was my grandson."

She hung her head in shame. "But I denied him. I was sure that if my daughter knew John was dead she'd give up, and I didn't want her to die. And John was already dead, so it couldn't matter to him. So I lied. I said that it wasn't John, and that he had called us a few days ago to tell us that someone had stolen his wallet.

"The police believed me." Mrs. Coltrain took a deep breath. "I've always felt guilty about what I did. But even so, I'd do it again because my daughter lived another five months. So you see, no one knows about what happened to John." She held out the birth certificate to Kynan. "If you want to use this, I would be honored."

"The honor would be mine," Kynan said as he took the paper.

Nine

Jenna stared down at the list of artifacts she was supposed to be updating, trying to concentrate. She couldn't. Her mind simply refused to focus on broken pottery.

Surreptitiously, she watched Kynan as he paced across her living-room floor. His features were set in grim lines and the tension hovering around him was almost visible.

He suddenly broke off his pacing, went to the front door, opened it a crack and peered out.

"Is Macintosh out there?" she asked.

"No. We can't seem to attract anyone." He glared at the small black box sitting in the middle of the coffee table. During the three interminable days Kynan had been monitoring it, it had remained stubbornly silent. Only the pleasure of the intervening nights had made the wait bearable.

"It hasn't been very long." Jenna offered what comfort she could.

"Long enough. We should have heard something by now."

Jenna chewed on her lower lip uncertainly. Should she suggest that he wasn't getting an answer because there was no one out there to hear him? Or should she let him hang on to hope as long as he could? There was a great deal of truth to that saying about hope deferred making the heart grow bitter.

Jenna took a deep breath and blurted out, "Kynan, have you considered that they may not have survived the trip?"

Kynan winced as a burning shaft of pain lanced through him, making him feel giddy. Oh, he'd considered it, all right. That particular nightmare had nibbled at the edge of his mind since his first moment of full consciousness in the cave. But he refused to believe that fate could be so unkind. Or so capricious.

He looked over at Jenna. Her eyes were shadowed. Shadowed with worry about him, he realized. But she couldn't be any more worried than he was himself. His gaze dropped lower to her soft, pink lips and a sudden compulsion to kiss them seemed to pull him toward her.

He sank down on the sofa beside her and gathered her into his arms. Her body was warm and yielded against his tense frame. The feel of her soothed him, pushing back his growing sense of panic.

Kynan's grip tightened as she snuggled closer, nuzzling her face against his neck. He pressed his cheek against the top of her head. Her hair felt silky and smelled faintly of flowers. He closed his eyes and breathed deeper, savoring the fragrance. Her scent triggered memories of springtime in Atlantis. Of fields of wildflowers growing as far as the eye could see. Bright golds and soft pinks and glistening whites and muted blues and regal purples, all tangled up in the verdant green grasses.

He squeezed his eyelids together, trying to hold on to the scene. People he knew were walking through those fields, laughing and talking to each other. A wave of homesickness that was a physical ache gnawed at him.

He wanted to be there. Walking once again with his friends. He wanted—Jenna wasn't there, he realized suddenly. Those people he remembered didn't include Jenna, and without Jenna . . . The image of what had been, began to fade beneath the reality of Jenna in his arms. There wasn't anyone he remembered who meant one tenth as much to him as Jenna did.

"Suppose they don't come?" Jenna persisted.

"If they don't . . ." Kynan couldn't make himself finish the thought.

"Come." Jenna did it for him. "How long do you intend to wait for them?"

"How long does one wait for rescue?" he asked heavily.

"Kynan, you are not some helpless creature who needs to have someone else rescue you from a situation you think is intolerable."

"It *is* intolerable!"

Jenna tilted her head back and stared into his taut features. The green had entirely leached out of his eyes, leaving them a dull blue. He looked . . . frantic, she thought uneasily. Maybe she shouldn't push now. Maybe she should wait. But it was the expectation that he was going to be able to leave the earth that was causing him to not face the situation. And facing it couldn't be as bad as pinning your whole future on something that wasn't going to happen.

"Am I intolerable?" she asked.

Kynan's eyes widened, taking on a greenish tinge. "Certainly not! You are unique. In both my world and yours."

"Unique is not necessarily good."

"Believe me, Jenna Farron, to me you are the epitome of everything a woman should be." The conviction in his voice warmed her. "You're intelligent and compassionate and sexy. In fact—" the greenish gleam in his eyes seemed to grow as she watched "—you are the sexiest woman I have ever met."

Kynan nuzzled the soft skin behind her ear, and she shivered, snuggling closer to him. "I find you a constant delight to hold and positively intoxicating to kiss." He lowered his head and captured her lips. His mouth felt firm and warm and infinitely exciting against her own.

Twisting slightly, Jenna wrapped her arms around his neck. She threaded her fingers through his hair, savoring its rough-silk texture. She could feel the tension beginning to build deep within her. It coiled tighter and tighter as his tongue surged into her mouth.

Tremors raced along her nerve endings, landing in her mind where they exploded into puffs of silvery sparks.

A shrill, whining noise suddenly ripped through the gossamer veil of happiness surrounding her and bludgeoned her eardrums.

Kynan jumped to his feet and sprinted across the room. He grabbed the black box and pressed something. The sound abruptly ceased.

"Mercy!" Jenna rubbed her forehead. "That thing could be a weapon. What happened? Did it malfunction?"

"No," Kynan muttered, his whole attention focused on the box.

Curious, Jenna peered over his shoulder to see what he found of such interest. To her surprise, there were tiny red dots skipping across the dull black surface, moving from right to left before they winked out of existence. There seemed to be a pattern to them.

Her sense of unease grew at Kynan's triumphant expression.

"What is it?" she asked.

"Our answer," he said, never taking his eyes off the moving lights.

Jenna blinked uncomprehendingly. An answer? She examined his words. Surely he didn't mean ... A sinking feeling dropped into the pit of her stomach, making her queasy. *Kynan had gotten an answer?* She repeated the words, but they were no more acceptable the second time around. Or believable. If he'd really gotten an answer, it had to mean that...

She hurried over to the patio doors and looked up into the painfully bright afternoon sunlight. The only things visible in the pale blue sky were streaky filaments of white clouds. Nothing else. No airplanes, no helicopters, and no flying saucers.

Of course, there were no flying saucers, she assured herself. She was simply off-balance from Kynan's kiss or she would never even have considered the idea.

Kynan's machine had probably just picked up on someone's transmission. The airwaves were crammed with signals from people and governments with something to say. That was what it was. It could even be Macintosh sending out a signal to try to trap them.

Despite the fact that they hadn't seen him since he'd tried to arrest Kynan, Jenna didn't for one moment believe he had really given up. She shivered as she remembered the determined gleam in his eye. Sooner or later, the colonel would be back. Of that she was positive.

"The pattern is repeating now." Kynan set the box back down on the table and hurried to the front door to check the street.

Jenna watched him, not certain what to say. He really seemed to believe that the signal had come from his compatriots.

"What did it say?" she finally asked.

"I'm not sure," he conceded. "The code isn't one I recognize, but they did respond and they'll undoubtedly send someone to investigate, so we'd better get out to the transmitter because that's where they'll come."

"Kynan..." She paused, trying to figure out how to tell him not to be too credulous without sounding patronizing. "What if the message is a fake? Suppose your signal was intercepted by some governmental agency, and they decoded it and then sent you a message to lure you out to the transmitter so they can capture you?''

Kynan shook his head. ''They couldn't have sent the signal because your culture hasn't yet discovered that type of transmitter wave.''

''You can't know that! Simply because it isn't common knowledge doesn't mean that it isn't known somewhere by someone.''

''It isn't possible,'' Kynan insisted.

Jenna bit her lip in frustration. She didn't know whether he really, truly believed what he was saying, or if he simply wanted to believe it. Either way, it spelled trouble. They could be walking straight into a trap. Ah, well, she thought fatalistically. She couldn't think of anyone she'd rather walk into a trap with.

''We have time to say goodbye to Mrs. Coltrain,'' Kynan said. ''Let's go see if she's home.''

The visit with Mrs. Coltrain helped to restore Jenna's sense of equilibrium. She still thought Kynan was walking into a trap, but she was no longer so sure the government could spring it. After all, she had a perfect right to be in the desert. In fact, that was her normal mode of behavior. There was no real way the government could tie that transmitter to her and Kynan. Any good lawyer could get the case laughed out of court. And she knew lots of good lawyers; she comforted herself with the thought of the law school at her university. They'd relish taking on the government.

Jenna smiled absently at something Mrs. Coltrain said and went back to considering the situation from all angles. This might turn out to be a blessing in disguise, she finally decided. Maybe this would convince Kynan once and for all that there wasn't anyone out there. Then they could begin to make plans for the future.

The future... Jenna remembered how long a future Kynan had with a feeling of sadness. If only it was possible that his restorative could have worked and they could have had all

hat time together. But common sense as well as science told
er that no potion could change one's physical makeup to
hat extent. It was bad enough that Kynan was chasing a
ipe dream. She at least should face reality. But even though
he was destined to be only a memory in his long life, she
vas determined to be the best memory he ever had.

"It was so nice of you to come for coffee." Mrs. Col-
rain's voice pulled Jenna out of her thoughts, and she
miled warmly as the old woman got to her feet.

"The pleasure is mutual," Kynan assured her.

Mrs. Coltrain unexpectedly giggled, sounding seventy
years younger. "You mean it's not my cookies you come to
at?" She glanced down at the plate of brownies Kynan had
een devouring.

Kynan suddenly looked uncertain. "Have I committed a
social solecism?" he asked Jenna.

"No," Mrs. Coltrain answered him. "I was just teasing
you. I forgot that you're a foreigner. I consider it a compliment to my cooking. Do come again," she urged as she
walked them to the door.

To Jenna's relief, Kynan didn't tell Mrs. Coltrain that he
couldn't because he'd booked passage "off-world" that
evening.

"Take care," Mrs. Coltrain called after them as they left.

Jenna peered up and down the street before crossing.
"Still no Macintosh."

"So it would seem," Kynan agreed. "Come on, let's go."
He opened the garage door and gestured her into the truck.

It wasn't until about six blocks later that Jenna realized
that she'd been overly optimistic. She checked her rearview
mirror as she was getting ready to pass a slow-moving van
and felt a sudden clutch of fear as she caught sight of a white
car with an emblem on its side a few hundred yards behind
them. She instinctively pulled over into the slow lane, hoping that she'd been mistaken. That it wasn't really Macin-

tosh. That it was simply someone in a car like his and that the car would pass them.

"What's wrong?" Kynan asked.

"I'm not sure, but I think..." She checked her rearview mirror again. The white car had also slowed down. It was being very careful to keep pace with her.

Kynan turned and looked out the rear window. "Macintosh," he said flatly. "By himself."

Jenna smacked the palm of her hand on the steering wheel in frustration. "Of all the dumb luck! He wasn't there when we left. He must have just arrived and seen us leaving."

"Hmm." Kynan continued to watch Macintosh's car, a thoughtful expression on his face.

Jenna took a deep breath. "Well, we've lost him before. We'll just have to do it again."

"Go ahead and try."

Jenna glanced curiously at Kynan, wondering at the abstracted note in his voice. Was it because of Macintosh's sudden appearance or was it because he was nervous over what he thought was the coming meeting with his fellow Atlanteans? Probably the latter, she decided as she suddenly swung into a side street, leaving Macintosh stuck at the intersection.

She backtracked through a series of winding subdivision streets and fifteen minutes later emerged on a main road with no sign anywhere of Macintosh.

"There," she said. "That took care of him." Unfortunately, her feeling of triumph was short-lived. Ten miles out of town, when the heavy traffic cleared, Jenna once again checked her rearview mirror and a feeling of frustrated disbelief shafted through her.

"Damn!" she said.

Kynan didn't even bother to check behind them. "Macintosh, I take it?"

"I wish someone would take the blasted man! I would have sworn that we lost him in that subdivision."

"You probably did. I would say that our colonel is a man who learns from his mistakes."

"Well, tell me so I can learn, too," Jenna muttered as she sped up. It didn't help. Macintosh matched her speed, not gaining and not falling behind.

"At a guess, I'd say that he put a homing device on your truck, and he's tracking the signal it sends out."

Jenna grimaced. "So much for my fancy footwork in the subdivision."

She glanced on either side of the road. As far as she could see there was level ground covered with short tufts of grass, cactus and stunted shrubs. There was no place for anything bigger than a prairie dog to hide. Certainly no place to conceal a truck while they searched for the tracking device.

"Now what?" she asked.

"We have no choice. We lead him to the rendezvous and if he tries to interfere..."

They did, too, have a choice, Jenna thought grimly. They could always listen to the voice of reason and give up this idiotic trek into the unknown.

A feeling of frustration filled her. How could her life have become so complicated in such a short period of time? But some of those complications were rather spectacular, she reminded herself. She had discovered a whole new world of sensation. What she had with Kynan was worth protecting by whatever means she had at her disposal. Determinedly, she continued driving, doing her best to ignore the colonel.

An hour later, Jenna pulled the truck off the winding road she'd been following for the last fifteen minutes and cut the engine. The cloud of dust a quarter of a mile behind them signaled Macintosh's whereabouts.

She tapped her fingers on the steering wheel and tried to plan. The problem was she didn't know what she was planning for. She carefully scanned the foothills beside the road. About half a mile on the other side of them was where they'd planted Kynan's transmitter. But what else lurked there besides the transmitter?

She turned and watched as Macintosh came to a halt about a hundred yards behind them. Was he trying to drive them into a trap?

"I wonder how many of his friends we'll find waiting there?" She gestured toward the transmitter.

"Probably none. Look." Kynan pointed to the ground around the truck. "There are no fresh tire tracks. There's only the tracks we made when we brought the transmitter. And no one could have come in from the other side because of the mountains."

"True. Flying a helicopter into those mountain currents would be asking for trouble." Her spirits lifted fractionally and then plummeted when she remembered that Kynan had received an answer. He couldn't be right, could he? The appalling thought momentarily shook her, but innate common sense quickly steadied her. There was no such thing as visitors from the stars. No one had ever found any evidence of them and heaven knew, enough people had looked. No, a far more likely scenario was that someone had managed to intercept Kynan's transmission and had replied on the same frequency.

Jenna took a deep breath and shoved the truck's keys into her jeans pocket. Sitting here speculating was useless. All she had to do was trudge over those mountains and she'd know for sure.

"We'll get the gear out of the back and act as if we're just looking for artifacts," she proposed. "If Macintosh or anyone else tries to stop us, that's our cover story."

She scrambled out of the truck, nervousness making her movements jerky. Kynan followed more slowly, his attention centered behind them where Macintosh was getting out of his car.

Kynan accepted the box of equipment she handed him. "Look." He nodded toward Macintosh.

Jenna stole a quick glance at the colonel, who was leaning up against his car's front fender, watching them. This was ridiculous, she thought. Here they were, the only three people in sight and they were studiously pretending they were alone.

"I see the blasted man!" she muttered.

"Do you also see the thing he has strapped to his waist? It is a gun, is it not?"

Jenna's head snapped around and she took a good look at the colonel. Sure enough, in a holster strapped around his waist was a large black revolver. An icy trickle of fear slithered down her spine. Guns were not funny. Not in any way, shape or form. They were dangerous, especially in the hands of a fanatic, which she strongly suspected Macintosh was. There was no telling what he might do if he were to feel threatened. He might even decide to simply shoot them first and try to explain his actions later.

Jenna swallowed on the lump of fear that clogged her throat and tried to think, but her mind seemed to be operating in slow motion. All she wanted to do was scramble back into the truck and get the hell out of there while she still could.

She turned to Kynan who was watching Macintosh with grimly set features. He wouldn't go. She knew it. Nothing on earth would convince Kynan to leave. And she couldn't leave him to face whatever might happen by himself.

She couldn't leave him because she was in love with him. The knowledge bubbled up from the depths of her being. She couldn't leave Kynan because she loved him. She repeated the words to herself, examining them for flaws, and found none. It was the truth. A truth that she probably would have recognized much earlier if she had had a little more experience with the emotion.

Jenna stared at Kynan, her eyes lingering on the way the fierce desert sunlight was splintered into shards of light in his golden hair. She loved him. The words sounded better every time she repeated them. She loved his brilliant, inquiring mind; his warm, caring personality and his dry sense of humor. She also loved the way he made her feel. As if she were of infinite value.

It didn't make a great deal of sense that in such a short period of time, Kynan should have become the center of her universe, but the fact remained that he had. It didn't matter that she didn't know how deep his feelings for her went. All that mattered was that she loved him and she'd willingly risk anything and everything to protect him.

Kynan was the only man she had ever met who had seen her as a person first and an intellect second, and she loved him for it. She straightened her shoulders, hugging her love to her like a shield. She didn't know what was about to happen, but whatever it was, it wasn't too great a price to pay for having known Kynan. Kynan had shown her that she was more than a competent professional. She was also a woman capable of feeling extravagant emotions.

Determinedly, Jenna turned her back on Macintosh and nodded toward the location of the transmitter. "What's the quote? 'Into the valley of death rode the six hundred'?"

Kynan chuckled and the sound echoed richly in the still, hot air. "I never heard it, but knowing your culture, they probably all got killed."

Jenna smiled in spite of her fears. At least Kynan sounded blessedly normal. "Come on, let's go." She headed up the slope of the hill in front of them, being careful not to look back. When she reached the crest, she paused and, using the excuse of catching her breath, peered down into the gully where they'd secreted the transmitter. It was not visible from where they stood. But to her infinite relief, neither was anything or anyone else. There were no people and no machines. Nor were there any signs in the dirt that they had been there. The area looked exactly as it had when they'd left it.

Kynan took off his hat and stared up into the empty sky. 'From the strength of the signal I received, they shouldn't be far away. With luck, we should only have an hour or so to wait.''

And what would Kynan do when the hour came and went and no saucer landed? Jenna wondered. Wait another hour? And then another. They had a good five hours before the sun went down and the desert's night creatures came out. Maybe by then Kynan would be willing to admit that no one was going to come. She stifled a sigh. If that was what it took to convince him, then that was what it took. In the meantime, she might as well use the time to good advantage.

"Since we're going to have to wait, you can help me dig. And keep a sharp eye out for snakes and scorpions.'' She started down the hill, being careful where she stepped. The footing on the loose shale was treacherous and she didn't want to end the day by breaking something.

She stopped at the head of the gully. "This looks like a likely spot. You can start there.''

Kynan obediently picked up a tool and began to meticulously scrape away the top layer of dirt.

Jenna hunched down beside him and tried to focus on what she was doing. She found it hard to concentrate on anything except the fact that Macintosh was skulking somewhere on the other side of the hill, but she doggedly kept at it.

Almost an hour later she was explaining to Kynan the possible significance of the markings on the flat rock he'd unearthed when Macintosh suddenly darted out from behind the boulders to their left.

Jenna blinked at the sight of the gun he had leveled at them. Fear mixed with honest anger surged through her. How dare he hound them like this?

"Put your hands up,'' Macintosh ordered.

"Don't you know anything but clichés?'' Jenna snapped.

A flush stained Macintosh's lean cheeks as he walked slowly toward them. "If I were you, I'd keep my mouth shut, lady."

"If you were me, you'd have better sense than to harass citizens minding their own business!" she retaliated.

"That's enough!" he barked. "It won't wash anymore. I saw your signaling device." He gestured with the gun, and Jenna's eyes followed it in unwilling fascination. She glanced over at Kynan to find him watching Macintosh. There was no fear in Kynan's face. Just annoyance. She wasn't sure if that was good or bad. Kynan might command a superior technology, but that gun Macintosh was waving around could be very dangerous.

"It's not like anything I ever saw before, and I've seen plenty," Macintosh muttered with a nervous look over his shoulder.

Was he expecting visitors, too? Jenna bit back a hysterical giggle. It promised to get rather crowded around here.

"That transmitter must be what the drug cartel uses to interfere with our radar," Macintosh said. "And I want to be out of here before they deliver the next shipment."

"So leave," Jenna said flatly. "I certainly don't have any desire to prolong my acquaintance with you."

"Oh no, lady." Macintosh pointed the gun at her. "You're my ticket to the future."

"I think not." Kynan's dispassionate voice sent a chill through Jenna. Please, God, don't let Kynan try anything stupid, she prayed.

"Oh? And how do you intend to stop me?" Macintosh turned to Kynan.

"I was hoping that the law might interfere with what is clearly kidnapping," Jenna hurriedly inserted.

"I'm arresting you!" Macintosh corrected.

"You have no authority to arrest anyone," Jenna said, hoping it was true. "Especially not two people on private property doing what they have been given permission to do."

"Start moving toward my car." Macintosh moved closer to them. "Or I'll—"

Jenna's eyes widened in surprise as his gun suddenly flew out of his hand, landing a good thirty feet from where he was standing. Kynan's crystal, she suddenly remembered.

"Why, you..." Macintosh rushed at Kynan, who hit him across the base of the neck with the edge of his palm. The colonel went down like a rock.

Jenna gulped, staring at Macintosh's prone body. He looked so still. "He isn't... You didn't..."

"Of course not." Kynan took a length of thin rope out of her tool kit and tied up Macintosh with an efficiency Jenna could only admire. At least she'd admire it if she weren't so sure it was the first step on the road to a prison sentence. Maybe they could convince the judge that they thought Macintosh was a nut who was threatening them. It was certainly true enough.

"What are you doing?" she asked, as Kynan hefted Macintosh onto his shoulders.

"We'll put him over there in the shade by the transmitter. He'll get sunstroke if we leave him out here in the open."

If they waited until Kynan's visitors from space showed up, Macintosh would be more likely to expire of old age, Jenna thought glumly as she trailed along behind them.

Kynan carefully set the colonel down, and Jenna jammed Macintosh's hat back on his head. "Under other circumstances, I might have liked him," Kynan said.

"Not me." Jenna sat down across from Macintosh so she could watch him. "I can't stand officious men. Especially not officious men who get hold of the wrong end of the stick."

And she wasn't all that keen on obsessed ones at the moment, either, she thought as Kynan walked over to the transmitter and began to check the dials on the machine. She wiggled, trying to find a more comfortable spot. This could be a long, hot, uncomfortable wait. Unfortunately, the level of Jenna's discomfort increased significantly when Macintosh returned to consciousness a few minutes later.

"You aren't going to get away with this!" He glared at her.

Jenna glared back. "Get away with what? Trying to mind my own business? You're the idiot who came chasing after me, waving a gun like a refugee from a John Wayne movie. I intend to file a formal complaint with the police when I turn you over to them."

Jenna saw the flicker of doubt in his eyes and was encouraged. So Macintosh wasn't as sure of himself as he let on. Maybe she could pull this off, after all. With her playing the part of the wronged academic and with Kynan having Mrs. Coltrain's grandson's birth certificate, they had a fighting chance.

"If you're so innocent, what's Polanski doing down there?" Macintosh nodded toward Kynan, who was fiddling with the transmitter.

"He's curious. You pointed the thing out, and he's trying to find out what it does."

"It sends a signal—as if you didn't know."

"I didn't," Jenna said wryly. "Kynan's the one who finds machines fascinating. I still haven't figured out how to program my VCR."

"I tell you it's a signaling device."

Jenna shrugged. "You can tell me anything you want. I really don't care. I'm only interested in the past and that thing is all too new."

"It'll—" Macintosh broke off as a wave of crushing pain hit his chest with the force of a blow. For a moment he couldn't breathe.

"What's the matter?" Jenna asked worriedly, not liking the bluish tinge around his lips. "Do you have a heart problem?" she demanded.

"No!" He bit the word off as if he found the question mortally offensive.

"How about a drink of water, then," Jenna tried. "This heat is enough to make anyone feel faint. I'll be right back." She got to her feet and sprinted over to their equipment pack, intent on getting him some liquid as soon as possible.

She was carefully holding the water bottle to Macintosh's lips when she suddenly realized he wasn't drinking. The water was pouring out of his mouth and dripping onto his dark green uniform, leaving an even darker stain. His eyes were huge in his ashen face. Jenna dropped the bottle and grabbed his shoulders, fearing he was dying.

"No," he muttered. "Look."

Jenna turned to see what he was staring at and froze. Despite the blistering sun and the suffocating quality of the superheated air, an icy chill feathered over her skin. She closed her eyes, counted to ten and looked again. It was still there.

A silvery thing about forty feet wide and sixty feet long was gliding toward them.

"No." She shook her head as if by refusing to acknowledge it, it would go away. "No," she repeated more strongly. "I do not believe in flying saucers."

"He seems to," Macintosh said harshly.

Jenna looked toward Kynan, who was standing beside the transmitter watching the thing with a longing that was almost tangible.

"What the hell is he?" Macintosh muttered.

"Who, not what!" Jenna snapped. "His name is Kynan." Getting to her feet, she hurried down the slope toward him. If they were choosing up sides, she chose Kynan.

"It's them!" Kynan gave her a wide grin and grabbed her hands in an exuberant gesture.

His words echoed through Jenna's head, gathering force as they went until they were actually painful. Kynan really had been answered. The obvious truth couldn't be denied any longer. Kynan's signal had been answered. His fellow Atlanteans really were out there in space somewhere.

And they would take Kynan away. Her knees almost buckled with the strength of the pain that lanced through her. Kynan would climb into that thing and go away to a supposedly saner world, and she'd be left here. Alone. Alone as she'd always been. But worse. She swallowed against the overwhelming sense of loss that gripped her. This time it would be far worse, because now she knew what it was like to love someone. To share thoughts and feelings and emotions. This time she'd know exactly what she was missing.

She bit down on the inside of her lip, hard enough to draw blood, in an effort to keep from bursting into tears. Kynan looked so happy. She forced herself to face the truth. This was what he wanted—to go with these people. And she loved him enough to help him.

"There." Kynan pointed to a door that had suddenly appeared in the side of the ship.

For an agonizing moment nothing happened, and then a man jumped out of the ship. He was quickly followed by three others.

Jenna stared at the one who appeared to be the leader. His shortly cropped hair was coal black and tightly curled, but his eyes were mirrors of Kynan's. That same gorgeous blue-green. And they contained the same impatience, Jenna thought, as the man barked out something in a language that meant nothing to her.

Nor to Kynan, she realized, as he tried to answer the strangers in what she assumed was the language of Atlantis.

The leader shook his head and said something to one of the men behind him. The man disappeared back into the ship and reappeared minutes later with a squat-looking device that he set down between the commander and Kynan.

A relative of the device Kynan had used in the bunker, Jenna realized when it translated the commander's words.

"You are Kynan of the House of Phelan?" the commander asked.

Kynan nodded. "I am, and you are?"

"Jacthren, commander of the scout station on Titan."

"The moon of Saturn?" Jenna blurted out.

Jacthren looked at her, then down at their clasped hands, and raised his eyebrows questioningly.

"This is Jenna Farron, who has been very helpful to me," Kynan said.

That's me, Jenna thought on a wave of black humor. Good old helpful Jenna.

"We have come in answer to your distress signal," Jacthren continued. "The council of New Atlantis has authorized me to offer you sanctuary on our world." He gave Jenna a considering look. "And if it be your wish, the female, also. There must be something she can do," he added carelessly.

Jenna felt hope roll over her in a tide. She didn't care that it was obvious that Jacthren didn't want her or that she'd be faced with a whole new world or that she'd be giving up everything she'd worked so hard to attain. The only thing that mattered to her was that she'd be with Kynan. She could far more easily adjust to losing her world than to losing him.

Kynan frowned as for the first time he thought beyond removing Jenna from this world. Thought about what it would mean to her. What would she do on New Atlantis? She was a respected teacher and researcher in her own world—a position she'd worked hard to earn. Would she be accepted on Jacthren's world for the unique person she was? Or would she always be the earth female? The thought chilled him. She deserved better than that. She'd earned better than that.

But to go without her... He stared at the ship. To climb into that and leave Jenna behind. To leave her bright smile, her sharp mind, her enthusiasm, her compassion, her love-making...

He couldn't do it. He faced the immutable fact. He couldn't survive without her. He didn't want to even try. It wouldn't be living; it would be existing. Like being in a state of emotional suspended animation.

Gently, he reached out and ran his fingertips over her dear face, savoring the velvety texture of her skin. He wanted her to be happy more than anything and he very much feared she wouldn't be, in Jacthren's world.

"You will be very welcome in New Atlantis, Kynan of the House of Phelan," an older man standing behind Jacthren declared. "Every historian in our world is clamoring to speak with you."

Kynan winced. Was that all he was to these people? An oddity from the past to be studied and wrung dry of information? He was more than that to Mrs. Coltrain. To her he was a distinct individual. He was even more than that to her cat.

No, Kynan reached the inevitable conclusion. He didn't belong to Jacthren's world any more than he belonged to Jenna's. But she belonged here and he loved her enough to stay. It wasn't all bad, he realized. Granted, a great deal of this world could use a personality reorientation, but some people appeared to be quite normal, even by his standards. If he were to focus his energies on them, on helping them to move the Earth toward a more peaceful direction...who knew what he and Jenna might not accomplish in a few hundred years?

"Thank you, but no," Kynan told Jacthren.

Jenna stared at Kynan with eyes that widened under the force of her pain. He didn't want to take her with him. She heard his rejection on a rising tide of despair. He didn't want her. He didn't want to take any reminders from her world, not even her. The knowledge bit into her mind like acid into silk.

"We will stay," Kynan said.

Jenna gulped, afraid to believe she'd heard him correctly through the whirling sound in her ears. He was going to stay here? But why? From the first moment she'd met him, he'd done nothing but count the seconds until he could escape, and now they were offering him a one-way ticket off Earth and he refused? It made no sense.

"You are sure?" Jacthren sounded as shocked as she was.

"Yes," Kynan said, feeling right about his decision. "I was desperate to reach you because in my eyes you were all that was left of Atlantis, but you are not. Not really."

The older man behind the captain nodded. "Very true, Kynan. You are the last of an old, old race. But the female's race—"

"Jenna," she muttered.

"Jenna," he corrected himself, "and we from New Atlantis are branches off that trunk. We also found that we could not return to the past."

"What do you mean?" Jenna's interest was caught.

"Shortly after Kynan was put into suspended animation, my ancestors left Earth in fifty ships. Of that fifty, only thirteen made it to their destination. Surviving on a hostile world was not easy. For a time we slipped back into chaos, and Earth became little more than a persistent legend. Finally, about two hundred years ago, we rediscovered space travel and came looking for our origins."

"But why don't we know about you?" Jenna asked.

The man shrugged. "Your civilization had also slipped back, and in our eyes you were little more than savages. We decided to put an outpost on Titan and wait to see how you developed."

"I see," Jenna said slowly, understanding. "That would explain a lot of things. I—"

She broke off at the sound of loose rocks tumbling down the hill. Macintosh! She had forgotten all about him in the shock of the ship's arrival. He was scrambling up the hill, his progress severely hampered by not being able to use his hands.

As Kynan took a step toward Macintosh, Jacthren took a small cylindrical tube out of his pocket and pointed it at the colonel. A thin beam of blue light shot across the space and engulfed Macintosh. He dropped lifelessly to the ground.

"What did you do to him?" Jenna yelled at Jacthren.

"Immobilized him for further study." Jacthren seemed taken aback by her reaction.

"Come, Jenna." The older man picked up the translating device. "I am Lytis, a healer. I will look at your friend."

"He isn't my friend." Jenna scrambled after him, leaving Kynan with the commander. "But since I did tie him up, I feel a certain responsibility for him."

"Do you normally tie up people?" Lytis asked curiously.

"Only when they point guns at me," she muttered.

"I see." Lytis's blue eyes twinkled beneath his bushy, golden brows.

When they reached Macintosh, she rolled him onto his back and began to ineffectively rub his cheek.

Lytis unclipped a small, flat box from his belt and pushed some buttons on it.

"What's that?" Jenna asked.

"It tells me about my patient's physical functions. For example..." He pointed it at her and studied the output. Frowning, he shook the device and tried again.

"What's the matter?" Jenna asked.

"It seems to be malfunctioning. According to this, your immune system is the same as ours, but that cannot be. Humans have a very ineffective immune system."

Jenna's eyes widened and for a second her mind went totally blank. Kynan's concoction had worked? It didn't seem possible, but Lytis's machine said it was. Kynan had been right about the Atlanteans being out in space—which she'd never for a minute seriously believed. Apparently he'd also been right about the restorative. Which meant that she had centuries and centuries to spend with Kynan. A feeling of euphoria washed through her, only to fade as she glanced down and saw Macintosh.

"Kynan gave me something to reactivate my immune system," Jenna told Lytis. "But what about him?"

She gestured toward Macintosh, and Lytis passed his device down the length of the colonel's body.

"What's wrong with him?" Jenna demanded as Lytis studied the symbols on the top of his box.

"Yes, what seems to be the problem with him?" Kynan asked, as he and Jacthren approached.

Lytis shook his head in dismay. "His heart is very damaged. I am surprised he is not already dead."

"It would certainly be convenient if he were to die," Jacthren observed with a detachment that chilled Jenna. "If he recovers, he is not going to be quiet about what he has seen here."

No, Macintosh wouldn't be, Jenna conceded unhappily. If the colonel lived, he'd blab this all over. But would anyone believe him? Someone might, and if the authorities were to start digging into Kynan's identity as Mrs. Coltrain's grandson, they might discover the truth. But if they let Macintosh die to suit their own convenience, what kind of life could she and Kynan have, knowing it was founded on another man's death?

"In my time we had machines that could selectively erase memories," Kynan said slowly. "Has that technology been lost?"

"Not exactly," Lytis said. "Our version is not very reliable. We might miss a thread, and he will remember that." He shrugged. "I would not want to risk it myself."

"Well, then, what about simply erasing, say, the last month from his memory?" Jenna asked. "Can you do that?"

Lytis nodded. "Easily. It never fails."

"And since we are in effect robbing him of one month of his life we have to make amends," Jenna said.

"Your female reminds me of the women to be found on Sires Three, Kynan," Jacthren observed. "They can argue a man out of everything he owns and make him think they are doing him a favor by taking it."

Jenna ignored him. "Lytis, can you fix his heart? That would give him years of life in exchange for a month's memories."

"And I suppose you wish me to fix his clogged arteries and the faulty gene that caused the problem in the first place while I am at it?" Lytis said wryly.

Jenna nodded happily. "Yes, that's what I want."

"It seems like a lot of trouble to go through for an organism that will die in fifty years or so," Lytis argued.

"Not if you're the organism," Jenna said.

"Take him aboard and do it, Lytis," Jacthren ordered and then turned to Kynan. "When the human is repaired, we will return him to his vehicle and watch until he wakes up to make sure he is safe."

"Thank you." Jenna beamed at him. She was going to get Kynan, and their happiness was not going to be bought with another man's life. Not only that, but her future had just expanded from forty to fifteen hundred years.

"We have finished loading Kynan's truck, Jacthren." A man called up to him from the spaceship, bringing Jenna back to Earth with a bump.

"Loading what?" Jenna asked apprehensively. From what she'd seen, Atlantean artifacts were nothing but trouble.

"Just some things I wanted," Kynan answered her. "Mostly tracking devices so we can find out what happened to the other sites."

Jenna felt a surge of anticipation. If they could somehow manage to locate the historical archives . . .

"If you should wish to make contact with us, you now have a much more efficient means, Kynan," Jacthren told him. "And I will relay your offer to our historians. For now, I bid you farewell. Jenna." He gave her a courtly bow that reminded her of knights and dragons.

"What offer?" Jenna asked as she watched Jacthren and Lytis carry the colonel into their ship.

"I told Jacthren that we would welcome visits from their historians." Kynan suddenly swung her up into his arms and dropped a hard kiss on her lips. "Ah, Jenna, my beloved."

"Am I?" she asked wistfully.

"Yes," he said simply. "You're the light of my soul, and I will never be complete without you."

"We could still go with them," she offered. "I love you to distraction, and I don't care where we are as long as you're there, too."

"I wish we were alone back at the house." He stared down at her, frustration seething in his eyes. "I want to make love to you."

"Soon." She smiled happily at him.

"Soon," he agreed. Taking her hand, he started toward the truck. "Let's go. There's a whole world out there for us to enjoy."

Us. Jenna savored the word and found it infinitely satisfying.

*   *   *   *   *

COMING NEXT MONTH

Take 4 bestselling love stories FREE

Plus get a FREE surprise gift!

Silhouette

SPECIAL EDITION ™

It's our 1000th Special Edition and we're celebrating!

Join us these coming months for some wonderful stories in a special celebration of our 1000th book with some of your favorite authors!

Diana Palmer   **Nora Roberts**
Debbie Macomber   **Christine Flynn**
Phyllis Halldorson   **Lisa Jackson**

mini-series by:

Lindsay McKenna, Marie Ferrarella, Sherryl Woods, Gina Ferris Wilkins.

And many more books by special writers.

And as a special bonus, all Silhouette Special Edition titles published during Celebration 1000! Will have **double** Pages & Privileges proofs of purchase!

Silhouette Special Edition...heartwarming stories packed with emotion, just for you! You'll fall in love with our next 1000 special stories!

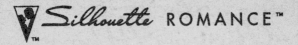

Silhouette ROMANCE™

Silhouette Romance presents the latest of Diana Palmer's
much-loved series

Long Tall Texans

COLTRAIN'S PROPOSAL
DIANA PALMER

Louise Blakely was about to leave town when Jebediah Coltrain made
a startling proposal—a fake engagement to save his reputation! But
soon Louise suspected that the handsome doctor had more on his mind
than his image. Could Jeb want Louise for life?

Coming in September from Silhouette Romance. Look for this
book in our "Make-Believe Marriage" promotion.

Become a
Privileged Woman,
You'll be entitled to all these Free Benefits.
And Free Gifts, too.

To thank you for buying our books, we've designed an exclusive FREE program called *PAGES & PRIVILEGES*™. You can enroll with just one Proof of Purchase, and get the kind of luxuries that, until now, you could only read about.

BIG HOTEL DISCOUNTS

A privileged woman stays in the finest hotels. And so can you—at up to 60% off! Imagine standing in a hotel check-in line and watching as the guest in front of you pays $150 for the same room that's only costing you $60. Your *Pages & Privileges* discounts are good at Sheraton, Marriott, Best Western, Hyatt and thousands of other fine hotels all over the U.S., Canada and Europe.

FREE DISCOUNT TRAVEL SERVICE

A privileged woman is always jetting to romantic places.

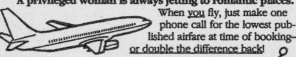

When you fly, just make one phone call for the lowest published airfare at time of booking— or double the difference back!

PLUS—you'll get a $25 voucher to use the first time you book a flight AND 5% cash back on every ticket you buy thereafter through the travel service!

PROOF OF PURCHASE

Offer expires October 31, 1996

SD-PP59